Breakaway

Gold Hockey #5

Elise Faber

BREAKAWAY
BY ELISE FABER
Newsletter sign-up

BREAKAWAY
Copyright © 2019 Elise Faber
Print ISBN-13: 978-1-946140-34-0
ISBN-13: 978-1-946140-33-3
Cover Art by Jena Brignola

GOLD HOCKEY SERIES

Gold Cast of Characters

Heroes and Heroines:

Brit Plantain (Blocked) — first female goalie in the NHL, loves boy bands

Stefan Barie (Blocked) — captain of the Gold

Sara Jetty (Backhand) — artist and figure skater

Mike Stewart (Backhand) —defenseman for the Gold, romance guru

Blane Hart (Boarding) — center for the Gold, number 22

Mandy Shallows (Boarding) — trainer and physical therapist

Max Montgomery (Benched) — defensemen for the Gold, giant nerd

Angelica Shallows (Benched) — engineer at RoboTech, also a giant nerd

Blue Anderson (Breakaway) — top forward in the league and for the Gold

Anna Hayes (Breakaway) — Max's former nanny, no relation to Kevin Hayes

Rebecca Stravokraus (Breakout) — Gold publicist, makes killer brownies, known at PR-Rebecca

Kevin Hayes (Breakout) — forward for the Gold, no relation to Anna Hayes

Rebecca Hallbright (Checked) — nutritionist for the Gold, plethora of delicious vegan recipes, known as Nutrionist-Rebecca

Gabe Carter (Checked) — doctor, head trainer for the Gold

Calle Stevens (Coasting) — assistant coach for the Gold, former national team member

Coop Armstrong (Coasting) — talented forward on the Gold, addicted to historical romance audiobooks

Mia Caldwell (Centered) — 5th degree black belt, brings the snark

Liam Williamson (Centered) — Gold forward finding his love for the game, charming and pushy in equal measures

Charlotte Harris (Charging) — new Gold GM, hates losing and the game Chubby Bunny

Logan Walker (Charging) — defensemen for the Gold, skills include: cockiness and being able to buy presents that make Charlotte squirm

Devon Scott (Block & Tackle) — former player, current owner Prestige Media group

Becca Scott (Block & Tackle) — Devon's assistant

Additional Characters:

Bernard — head coach

Richie — equipment manager

Dan Plantain — Brit's brother

Diane Barie — Stefan's mom

Pierre Barie — Stefan's dad, owner of the Gold

Spence — former goalie, married to Monique, daughter Mirabel

Monique — married to Spence, former model

Mirabel — daughter of Spence and Monique

Mitch — Sara's boss
Allison and Sean — Blane's parents
Pascal — Devon Scott's security lead
Roger Shallows — Mandy's dad
Grant and Megan — Devon's parents

ONE

BLUE

Blue walked into his teammate, Max's, backyard, his latest girl on his arm.

He'd met her at the bar last night, and they'd fucked like rabbits until the sun came up. Then they'd fucked some more.

Now, he was making the requisite appearance at Max's engagement party.

He was happy for his friends . . . for all of them.

But *fuck*, he was the last of the guys.

The final holdout.

The only single one.

Which wasn't really a fair assessment because there were other guys on the team who were single or divorced, but Blue wasn't that close to them.

Not like he was with Brit, Stefan, Blane, and Max.

They had been his people since his rookie season, and they'd taken him under their respective wings.

And now they were all married or engaged or had cute little babies.

Yes, he got that he was younger than them, knew that he had plenty of time to sow his wild oats and still have a family.

But all Blue knew was that it was getting damned old coming home to an empty house all the time.

"There are kids here," his date Bindi—or Bambi or Bobbi, because fuck if he could remember—said, and her tone told him she equated children with the seventh circle of hell.

"Yeah," he said. "The guys have a lot of kids."

Her face puckered with disgust, and suddenly Blue wasn't remembering how good of a hand job Bindi or Bambi or Bobbi could give, but how happy Angie had been when Max had proposed on the Golden Gate Bridge.

Blue wanted *that*.

Not *this*.

"You know what?" he said, taking Bindi or Bambi or Bobbi's hand in his and tugging her toward the front of the house, while he pulled out his cell with his other. "This will be lame. Why don't I text you later when I'm done?"

Calling the Über took seconds.

Untangling the octopus that was Bindi or Bambi or Bobbi upon the car's arrival took longer.

Much longer.

But finally, he managed to pack her into the car and sighed with relief as it drove away.

Until he turned and saw *her*.

Anna.

Who always looked at him with glarey eyes and a pissy expression.

"There's my Ice Queen," he said, moving past her and heading back to the party. He'd congratulate the couple then go the fuck back to his empty apartment.

"Doesn't it get old?" Anna asked, trailing after him.

"Doesn't *what* get old?" he countered, snagging a beer from a nearby table.

"Being a fucking sleaze."

Blue froze then shook his head. "You don't know me."

Anna rolled her eyes. "I know *plenty* of guys like you. Fuck anything that moves, never sleep with the same girl twice, and too wrapped up in your own damned cock to be a good lay."

She'd gotten his rage pretty ramped until the last statement.

That last one, though?

It tempered his anger.

He was good in bed. *Really* fucking good. In fact, Blue made it a point to make sure anyone he slept with had a better time than him. And that wasn't ego talking. Sex just wasn't fun for him if his partner didn't orgasm at least twice.

He was an overachiever. What could he say?

Ah. Now *there* was his ego talking.

Smirking, Blue tapped his chin. "Sounds like a personal problem to me. Maybe you're too cold in the sack to enjoy yourself. Or maybe you freeze a guy's cock off with your Ice Princess powers."

Anna huffed. "You're unbelievable, you know that?"

Blue jerked his chin toward the front of the house. "That's what *she* said."

As Anna flounced off, Blue couldn't stop himself from watching her ass, because as much as he teased her about being icy during their interactions, he had the feeling she was very much fire under all that frost.

Not that he'd ever find out.

He and Anna were oil and water, two tomcats fighting over territory or, metaphors aside, they just always managed to get on each other's nerves.

And while he couldn't deny she was hot and gorgeous, Blue wanted a little more peace in his life when he found the right woman.

He wanted a girlfriend who didn't constantly poke and antagonize but rather one who was sweet and gentle and kind. Like Sara.

Like Angie. Yes, that made him an egotistical asshole—that he wanted a pretty and nice girl at home—but there it was.

Blue had enough stress in his career that he wanted to keep it simple at home.

Who could fault him for that?

No one, dammit.

He snorted. Okay, *someone* could.

A gorgeous blond someone with a fantastic ass.

Blue smirked as he made his way to his friends, socializing for a while, making sure to stop by and congratulate the happy couple and wish them the best, playing with Max's son, Brayden, on the trampoline for a bit—which turned out to be a lot longer than a *bit* because once one kid saw him use the platform to launch Brayden in the air, Blue suddenly was begged and pleaded by all the kiddos to have a turn.

And then another.

So, by the time he dragged his tired ass off the trampoline, the party was breaking up.

He said his goodbyes and headed for the driveway, pulling out his cell for Über round two.

"Baby Blues." He turned, saw Anna getting into a Prius. "Need a ride?"

He raised his brows. "You going to freeze my balls off?"

A sexy smile. "You know it."

"I think I'll take my chances with the Über."

"Chicken."

Blue rolled his eyes. "Seriously?"

"Buck-buck," she clucked. "Buck-buck-*buuuck*."

"You're unbelievable."

"You're a chicken." She sat down in the driver's seat, started to close the door.

Blue sighed, sought patience from heaven. It didn't matter what she said. He knew he wasn't—

His eyes drifted back over to her car, and she was looking at him with that annoying ass smirk. *Dammit.* "Fine," he grumbled and stomped over to her Prius, opening the door and dropping down into the passenger's seat with a huff.

"Was that so terrible?" she teased.

"The worst."

Anna flicked on the radio, filling the airwaves with classic rock. Which surprised him—he'd figured she would be more of a pop girl. But before he could ask her about it, she turned up the volume and backed out of the driveway.

He had to shout directions to his place over the noise, but that was probably her intention. And it wasn't like he lived far or that the route was complicated.

Hell, he should probably be grateful she'd saved him the extra aggravation of having to converse with her.

Ten minutes later, she pulled into his driveway and put the car into park.

Only then did she turn down the volume.

"Your humble abode," she said, sweeping a hand toward the little cottage tucked into a hillside south of San Francisco. It was ridiculously expensive and still mostly empty, but it was home and, as an Army brat, probably the most settled he'd ever been in his whole life.

"Yup," he said, reaching for the handle. "Thanks for the ride."

"Try not to go out and get a fresh bimbo to *ride* tonight. I hear STIs are on the rise in the city."

Blue sighed, turned back to face her. "Really?"

She shrugged, a smirk teasing the edges of her mouth, drawing his focus to the lushness of her lips. "Just watching out for Max's teammate."

He rolled his eyes. "Not hardly."

"Okay, how about I'm trying to prevent you from spreading STIs to the female populace?"

"I'm clean, and I'm smart," he told her. "Condoms all the way."

"Ew."

Except there was something about the way she said it that made Blue stiffen and take notice. Because . . . he stared into her eyes, watched as the pale blue darkened to royal, saw her lips part as she sucked in a breath.

Holy. Shit.

"You're attracted to me."

Her jaw dropped. "No fucking way," she said, too quickly, pink dancing on the edges of her cheekbones. "You're delusional."

Blue got close.

Real close.

Anna licked her lips.

And fuck it all, he kissed that luscious mouth.

Two

BLUE

She tasted like heaven.

And cake.

Okay, not the most intelligent statement, but in reality, Blue was lucky to have a single thought in his brain that wasn't *more* or *fuck* or *now*.

Anna shoved at his chest, tearing her mouth away. "What the hell do you think you're doing?" The question was angry, but her eyes were hot and her hands . . . well, they were tracing little circles over his pecs that made goose bumps rise all over his body, and his cock—

"Kissing you," he said, curling his hand around her nape and tugging her lips back to his.

Sweet. So *fucking* sweet.

He had the feeling it wasn't the cake, but rather, just Anna herself that tasted like ambrosia—a not-so-surprising fuck you to the entirety of the male population. *"See?"* her mouth seemed to say. *"I'm beautiful and smart and just the feel of my lips against yours is hotter than any of the women you've slept with in the last year."*

Or maybe ever.

And when her tongue swept into his mouth to tangle with his, he saw fucking stars.

Literal stars.

Except they weren't the result of pleasure.

Because his lips were torn from hers, those hands that had been massaging circles on his chest only moments before shoved hard, and his head collided with the passenger's side window.

Thunk!

And cue stars.

"Fuck," he gritted, cock throbbing nearly as bad as his skull, but before he managed to do more than blink against the pain, Blue suddenly found himself going ass over tea kettle onto the concrete of his driveway. "Wh-what the fuck was that?"

He rubbed a hand over his eyes, used his other to push himself to his feet.

Anna stood inches from him, chest heaving, indigo eyes flaring with heat.

Or maybe annoyance.

Or—

She crossed her arms. "Don't you ever do that again you fucking . . . you *fucking* asshole—" She turned, slammed the car door closed then rounded the hood, staring back at him as he stood there gaping at her like an idiot. "I—" Her teeth clicked closed, and she shook her head. "I don't know why you would d-do that."

Blue raised a brow. "Um. You're beautiful and—"

"What? You kiss every beautiful woman you meet?"

"No." He stepped toward her, resting his hands on the top of the car. "But I've been wanting to do that since the first time I saw you."

"You—" Anna shook her head again. "Couldn't."

"Anna," he said, "you're sex incarnate." When she made a scoffing noise, it was his turn to shake his head and state bluntly. "Big boobs, gorgeous ass, hips a man wants to grab on to. Not to mention bright blue eyes and kissable lips and a mouth that often spouts fire." His own mouth curved. "Fire is sexier than smoke, I can tell you that much."

Her brows pulled together into a frown—and he'd be lying if he'd said he hadn't thought more than once about kissing that adorable little crease away.

Of course, that had been before she'd shown any interest in him.

When she'd been off-limits.

Well, she should *still* be off-limits.

But . . . interest.

What interest, asshole? his inner conscience shouted. *Did you pluck the notion from her mind? Or maybe it was her "heated eyes" that clued you in so clearly?*

Blue's gut sank, twisting itself into knots. His mental keeper of morals was pesky and more than a little annoying, but in this case, it was also right. Anna *hadn't* expressed any interest in him, and he'd jumped the gun, crossed a dozen boundaries because—

"I don't even know what that means," she said, drawing him out of his head and back into their conversation. "Neither smoke nor fire is sexy." Her frown deepened, and Blue found himself having to clench his hands into fists so he didn't round the car and *show* her exactly what that meant.

He forced his fingers to flatten out. "My point is that no real man wants to be with a woman who's as substantive as smoke. He wants something that's tangible, something he can have a conversation with."

"Some . . . *thing?*" She pressed her lips into a flat line.

Uh-oh.

Blue swallowed. "That's not what I meant."

And why was he pushing this anyway? Hadn't he just been

thinking about wanting a woman who didn't bust his balls? Who didn't spit fire at him? For all intents and purposes, he should be bolting for his front door, hoping the kiss had been more smoke instead of heat.

Except . . . it *hadn't* been smoke. It had been chock full of heat.

And then there was the fact that he'd seen Anna be sweet.

She was amazing with Brayden and the rest of the kids from the team, fit right in with the wives and girlfriends, was kind and nice to everyone. Everyone, that was, aside from him.

Which probably had more to do with *him* than her, considering the first time he'd met her had been outside the rink when she was waiting to pick up Brayden after a game and he'd thought she was there for—

Well, *not* for child-related activities.

He'd been a douche.

She'd not given an inch.

And here they were.

"My point is," he continued when she just glared at him, "Tangible is better than someone who has rocks for brains and—" He broke off when her expression darkened. "I'm going to shut up now."

"Finally, something smart has come out of your mouth." She sighed and yanked open her door. "Especially because I think that you were going to equate tangible with whatever semi-attractive non-stupid female that's in front of you."

"You're far from semi-attractive."

Anna's glare faltered. "Don't say that."

He opened his mouth to . . . what? He wasn't sure. Perhaps, to say it again, to try to convince her that he thought she was beautiful. Or maybe, and probably more likely, to say something that would piss her off all over again.

"Why?" Figuring it was safest, Blue settled on the one word.

She bit her lip and ducked her head, looking more vulnerable than he'd ever seen her. Anna was capable, confident, had her shit together more than any other person he'd ever spent time with. Her appearing so fragile did something to his hard ass heart— made it pulse, made it ache, made it *feel*.

"Anna, sweetheart, why shouldn't I say you're beautiful?"

"Don't," she whispered. "D-don't say that."

His heart twinged again, and the unfamiliar ache had him lifting his hand to rub at the pang. And stupid as it was, Blue found himself walking around the front of her car, not stopping until he had to crouch down a little bit to meet her eyes.

Her gaze met his for the barest blip of a moment before darting away.

"Baby—"

She stiffened and snapped, "I'm not your *baby*." A sigh. "Just go inside already." Her fingers gripped the handle of the door, tugged.

Blue had caught the metal panel before he'd even realized he'd moved.

"Anna."

She yanked at the door.

"*Anna.*"

Another shake of her head, another tug.

"Sweetheart, you're beautiful." She didn't look at him, but he kept talking anyway. "It's the truth, but regardless of that or what I've been feeling these last months, I was out of line. I shouldn't have kissed you, shouldn't have assumed you wanted—" He broke off before shoring his spine, knowing at the very least, he owed her an apology. "It was wrong, and I'm sorry."

She froze, gaze tipping up to the sky, and he got the feeling she was talking more to herself than him. "We are not doing this. You are not doing this. *I* am not doing this."

Blue touched her cheek, drawing her eyes to his. "This isn't a line, and I'm not trying to play you, Anna. It's simply . . . indisputable fact."

Her lids slammed closed. "I am *not* doing this."

"Not doing what?" he asked.

A shuddering breath before her bright blue gaze met his. Pink stained her cheeks. Her tongue darted out and moistened her lips.

He'd been so focused on getting her to see reason, for her to understand that she was gorgeous, that he was sorry and wasn't playing some game with her, that Blue had almost forgotten how combustible that kiss had been.

But one glimpse of that pink tongue had heat raging back in.

"*This*," she said and launched herself into his arms.

THREE

She had to give him credit, Blue recovered quickly.

One second, she was standing on the ground, the next, she was in his arms, her legs wrapping around his hips, her mouth slamming onto his. And in another, he turned, used a foot to shut the car door, and slid his tongue between her lips.

Anna found her back pressed against the cool metal of her sedan, her front flush against the wonderful hardness that was Blue, and her breath stolen in a kiss that threatened to light her skin on fire.

She shouldn't be doing this.

She *couldn't* be doing this.

But the fucking man had been sweet and earnest and—

He did something with his tongue that made every coherent thought poof right out of her head.

She kissed him harder, slipping her arms around his shoulders, weaving one hand into the short locks on the back of his neck. She loved the bristles there, loved the way they felt against her fingertips. His mouth moved from her lips to her jaw to her earlobe, down her throat, nipping at her collarbone.

"We should stop," he rasped against her skin, the damp heat of his words making her shiver.

They should.

This was a recipe for disaster.

And yet . . . Blue knew nothing about her or her past. He didn't know why his words had touched her so deeply.

He'd just been nice and genuine and . . . he'd kissed her like he hadn't been able to get enough.

A man who wanted her for her.

Her fucking kryptonite. Pathetic, but there it was.

"We should," she agreed, but instead of backing away, instead of getting into her car and driving off, Anna grabbed Blue's head and tugged his mouth back down to hers.

One frozen moment before he groaned, hands sliding to her waist, lifting her up again so she straddled his hips, and then she was pressed right against the glorious hardness of his cock. *And glorious*? Fuck, but normally she'd be laughing at herself for using such a word. Penises were penises. They served their purpose, could occasionally bring her to orgasm.

Very occasionally.

But *Blue's* penis?

It deserved the term glorious, all big and hard and rubbing against the exact spot she needed.

"House," she said, breaking away from his lips to gasp in much-needed oxygen.

"We shouldn't—"

His words cut off when she arched against him, breasts pressing against his chest, hips tilting to get even closer.

"It's really fucking stupid," she said. "But, Blue, don't tell me that it wouldn't be good."

Heated eyes met hers. "Of course, it's going to be good."

Anna didn't miss the use of present tense in his statement. It made her shiver with anticipation then she stretched up to kiss him again.

"But—" he began when they broke apart for air again.

"Blue," she said, placing a finger over his lips. "I need an orgasm that's not courtesy of Bucky, my vibrator. I also need one that's not courtesy of a boyfriend." His tongue flicked out, caressed the tip of her finger, making her shiver again. "Don't over-think this," she whispered.

He peeled her hand away and bent, halting with his mouth mere centimeters from her jaw. His hot breath raised goose bumps on her skin. "But you hate me."

She didn't. She really didn't.

Anna was just really good at pretending she did because he was so fucking dangerous to her mental well-being. Because despite the string of women in and out of his bedroom, despite being more gorgeous than any man had a right to be, and *definitely* despite the fact that he seemed to revel in pressing every *single* button she possessed, Blue was one of the good ones.

He visited kids in the hospital, raised money to provide free sports equipment for underprivileged youth. And not one of the numerous women parading through his bedroom had ever said a bad word to the media.

The guys on the team loved him as did the wives and girl-friends and staff members.

Hell, *everyone* loved him.

The media had him slated to be the next captain.

The fans thought he could do no wrong.

It was terrible.

Well, for her self-control anyway. Especially when he did things like hospital visits and raising money for charity. During the last game she'd gone to, he'd paid for an entire team of ten-year-old female hockey players and their parents to attend, had bought them slushies and hot dogs—well, roast turkey sandwiches and beers for the adults—and had even given everyone Gold jerseys emblazoned with their last names.

Hence the hating.

It was safer that way.

"Yes," she said, tilting her head in invitation, while she lied her ass off. "I hate you. But hate sex is also good sex."

One side of his mouth curved into an arrogant smirk. "*Blue* sex is good sex."

"So many words," she countered. "So few orgasms."

The other half of his mouth curled up. "Last chance, sweetheart," he said.

"For what?" A careless shrug. "Me left wet and aching while you deal with performance anxiety?"

He growled, fingers tightening on her hips, teeth nipping at her jaw. "Had to push didn't you, sweetheart?"

"So. Much. Talk—"

She broke off with a squeal as Blue hefted her over his shoulder. Totally caveman, and she should probably turn in her feminist card for this, but she didn't completely hate it.

Especially when it afforded her such a fabulous view of his hockey player ass.

And hockey players had the *best* asses.

"I gave you a chance," he said. "Now, you're mine."

Anna's heart skipped a beat, and it wasn't just from the promise in his voice. No, it was because his words were possessive, filled with need.

God, she wanted that.

But she couldn't have it, so she shoved the emotion deep, reached her hands down to cup Blue's cheeks.

And not the ones on his face.

"Prove it, Anderson."

FOUR

His heart was pounding, his dick was granite, and his brain was screaming that this was a fucking horrible idea.

But Anna.

Beautiful Anna with all her sharp edges, the biting words, the flashing blue eyes . . . the great fucking ass.

Under his palm.

Her breasts, which were brushing his shoulder with every step he took.

Funny how quickly the voice in his head quieted.

He fished out his keys, unlocked the front door and pushed it open, then set Anna on her feet just outside the threshold. "Last chance."

She propped one hand onto her hip. "You said that already."

His dick twitched, and Blue stopped what minimal thinking he was doing. Instead, he swept Anna back up into his arms, stepped inside, and kicked the door closed with his heel. A nudge of his elbow slid the lock home.

And his mouth got busy, slanting across hers, tongue slipping between her lips, teasing and nipping and fucking enjoying the hell out of the way she tasted.

He'd planned to move down the hall, to get her into his bed, but she had different plans.

Her hands slipped down, past his waistband, straight for his—

Blue's knees went weak.

He went with it, sinking down on the rug in his hallway, tugging Anna down with him. He tore at the hem of Anna's shirt, yanked it up and over her head. Her breath caught as he nipped at her waist, her ribs, the delicate silken flesh spilling out of either side of her black, lacy bra.

"Blue," she panted, and fuck did he like his name on her lips. Seeing her all breathless, flush spreading down from her cheeks to her throat to her chest.

He wanted to lick every inch of it.

And he would.

But at the moment, he needed to focus on getting them both to orgasm as quickly as possible, to scratch the necessary itch, to get his control back, to make the most of this night together.

Because that was all they'd have.

One night.

One night to cram it all in, one night he could pretend was just a mistake, a mutual exchange of orgasms, one night that couldn't lead to more.

Because as beautiful and sexy and wonderful as Anna was, they weren't meant to be.

She shifted beneath him, one hand weaving into the hair on his nape.

"You okay, Big Guy?"

Blue blinked. *Fuck*. He needed to get his shit together. Because if this night was all they were going to have together, he was going to make it count . . . and also, he was going to ignore that *if*. This was it. A single night before he forgot about fire and heat and focused on sweet and warm.

Even if sweet and warm was suddenly as appealing as being traded to the Ducks.

Focus.

He never had a hard time concentrating in bed—or floor, rather. He treated fucking like it was his second job, an off-ice skill to hone and perfect.

But with Anna . . .

Well, it was different.

Her fingers tugged lightly, concern creeping into the edges of her expression and chasing away desire. "We don't have to—"

He let his hips drop more firmly on top of Anna's, cutting off her words.

"I—" She gasped when he tore the tiny strip of black lace holding the front of her bra together, but he didn't falter, just bent his head and sucked one nipple into his mouth. "*Blue.*" Her long moan made his dick ache.

He switched sides, soaking in her groans, hands stroking over every silken inch of her bare skin, before finding his way back to her mouth and kissing her until they were both gasping for air. Then he kissed her some more, fingers drifting down her side to undo the button of her jeans. This was hampered by the fact that Anna was doing the same to him, struggling with the fastening while at the same time fighting with the hem of his shirt.

Blue reared back and yanked it off then undid the button of his jeans and slid down the zipper.

Anna was panting—not that his breathing was all that steady either.

But the sight of her breasts bouncing in time to those rapid breaths had him freezing in place for a moment just to appreciate the view.

"Fuck," he growled. "I have got to get my mouth back on those."

Her hips jerked, and he grinned. "You like that, don't you?" he asked, reaching up to pinch one rosy nipple.

"Mmm." Hazy blue eyes met his, fire still in their depths. "You know I do." Kiss-reddened lips curved, and his cock somehow got even harder. Blue's heart rate was higher than when he got stuck on the ice for a long-ass shift, and yet . . . he was finally starting to feel like himself again.

He was in control.

And this was going to be really fucking good.

"Lift your hips, baby," he ordered, dragging his mouth down her throat, her cleavage, nipping just above one hip.

She complied, and he tugged her jeans down and off, taking the strappy sandals she wore off along with them.

More black lace.

Fuck him senseless.

Yes, he thought, reaching for the scrap of fabric and pulling it down. *That's the plan.*

He slid his fingers back up the insides of her thighs, sweeping closer to her pussy, loving that she spread her legs wider, that he could see all that pink glistening with moisture.

He bent, needing to taste, but Anna stopped him with a hand on his chest.

"Later," she said. "I need you inside me, Blue."

Desire twisted his gut, roughed the words coming out of his throat. "Yeah, you do," he said. "But we'll both just have to wait." He dove between her thighs, fingers spreading her wide and mouth latching onto her clit.

"*Oh fuck,*" she groaned.

He took a moment to find what she liked—firm pressure with his tongue, a finger inside that stroked her G-spot—and then set to work, harder and faster, bringing her up to the edge.

Normally, he might have stalled, keeping her there, teasing her with the tendrils of an orgasm, but Blue was too far gone, his control razor-thin at best.

So, he guided her right over the edge and didn't stop.

"Oh fuck. Oh fuck—" she chanted, head writhing from side to side, body stiffening and then softening and then stiffening again as he kept working his tongue and finger.

Only when she began clenching around him did he reach into his back pocket for his wallet to pull out a condom.

A heartbeat to push his jeans down past his hips, another to roll it on.

And then . . . fucking nirvana.

She was tight and hot around him, her mouth parted in a little O he was desperate to kiss off her lips.

So he did.

And then he moved.

Fuck, but she met him stroke for stroke, his orgasm barreling down on him, pleasure sliding down his spine, spiraling through his limbs. He pounded into her, not stopping as she lifted her legs up to wrap around his hips, just shifting his angle slightly so that her eyes widened and her back arched.

"Blue," she moaned. "Fuck. *Yes*. Don't—*oh God*—stop."

He couldn't stop. Wouldn't have been able to stop even if the world were ending.

"Come on, baby," he said, tilting his hips so he pressed more firmly against her clit. "Come for me."

Come before he embarrassed himself because—

Fuck.

His orgasm exploded through him, but—thank fuck—because Anna toppled over the edge alongside him.

"I can't feel my legs," she murmured what could have been hours or minutes later. She opened her eyes, lips curving up into a smirk when he leaned back to stop crushing her. "I blame that solid Gold cock."

And that right there.

That was what made her so fucking dangerous.

Because after the best orgasm of his life, he found himself laughing.

Laughing while sprawled on his hallway rug, ass out, dick still inside her.

Inside a woman he'd spent the last two seasons trying to convince himself was absolutely wrong for him.

Laughing with a woman he was afraid might shatter all of those carefully held expectations.

And then what would he do?

Ignoring the voice that said he might finally start living, Blue shrugged off the past, the emotions, pushed away everything except the beautiful woman beneath him. He smiled down at Anna and shifted so he could lift her into his arms.

"I got you," he assured her, when she gasped in surprised, then nipped at her earlobe. "By my count, you've got at least three more orgasms to go tonight."

Her mouth dropped open, and he slanted his lips across hers, kissing her deeply as he carried her down the hall to his bedroom.

This he could do. Kissing. Orgasms. Fucking.

Feeling too much for a person he couldn't have?

That was off the table.

And so Blue had circled back to *one night*.

Time to make the most of it.

FIVE

ANNA

She crossed her arms over her chest, glaring up at the man standing outside her front door.

And not the man she wanted to be standing there.

Dammit.

She was not supposed to be thinking about Blue. Or the empty space next to her on the mattress when she'd woken up in his bed. Or the fact that a coffee and bagel had been waiting for her on the kitchen counter, along with her car keys.

A clear signal that their moment was up. And paired with Blue's absence, a nice, but firm GTFO.

Also, a good reminder for her to not lose herself, no matter how incredible her multiple—yes, Blue *Fucking* Anderson had serious bedroom skills—orgasms had been.

And his mouth. And his cock—

Which was So. Not. The. Point.

"Is something wrong with Brayden?" she asked Max, shaking herself and pushing the images of the previous night deep, *deep* down.

Max shook his head.

She sighed, relaxing back against the doorframe. Because no matter that she'd resigned from her position as Brayden's nanny, the little boy had sewn himself deeply into her heart. He was hers, forever, even though she couldn't be *his* any longer. Brayden and Max had Angie, and they were busy forming their own family now.

"We talked about this already," she said. "You don't need me anymore."

Max frowned. "You're not fucking Mary Poppins. You don't have to disappear just because you think your job is done." He tugged the end of her ponytail. "You're part of the family, Anna."

Her heart squeezed.

Because she wanted that. So *freaking* much.

It was the one thing she had always wanted most in the world and also the one thing she desired that she would *never* admit to anyone.

To do that would make her vulnerable, and if Anna had learned anything in her twenty-nine *long-ass* years, it was that being vulnerable was dangerous to her heart and soul.

No, it was better to keep her distance, to keep those yearnings safely locked away.

Safer to have people relying on her and not the other way around.

"Max," she said. "I didn't set out to be a nanny my whole life. I want—" She bit back the rest of the words. It didn't matter what she wanted. It never had.

"What?" he murmured, reaching over to tip up her chin when she let her gaze drop to the ground. "What is it you want, kiddo?"

Anna's mouth curved. "I'm not a kiddo."

Max gave a chagrined smile. "I know. I'm sorry." A shrug. "Force of habit."

Considering, Anna had found herself calling strangers "kiddo" after getting so used to using it with Brayden, she couldn't be mad.

Hell, the other day she'd told her barista, "Thank you, bud," and the barista was a woman.

Autopilot was a real thing.

Which was also why she needed to make a clean break with Max.

Before they got too comfortable and used to each other, before they began to rely on one another—

No. Not *they*. Her. Before *she* did any of those things.

"Okay, *not* kiddo," he said. "Tell me what it is you want."

"I'm going back to school."

His face lit up. "That's great! I can—"

"No," she said. "You'll enjoy your fiancée and son—that's what you'll do."

"Anna. I'll pay—"

God, she loved this man. The older brother she'd never had, caring and sweet and a huge dork. "You already paid me a fortune. I can do this on my own."

He sighed, stared down at her. "I'm not going to change your mind, am I?"

She shook her head. "Nope."

"Stubborn." Another sigh. "But I know you've got this, Anna. You're fantastic at anything you put your mind to."

Her heart skipped a beat, but before she could open her mouth to poo-poo that notion, Max continued talking.

"You're smart, and I know you'll nail it." He grinned, probably because they both had an extreme fondness for the cooking competition show on Netflix of the same name. "What do you want to study?"

She bit her lip. "Elementary education." The big lug's eyes warmed, and Anna found her own getting a little misty. She swatted his chest. "Stop that."

Max pulled her into a hug. "I'm proud of you."

Her own arms tightened for just a second before she let go and stepped back. "I haven't even started yet."

"You'll finish." A beat of quiet, broken by the buzz of his phone. He tugged it out of his pocket, glanced down at the screen, and smiled. "Angie says if you won't come back then you at least have to promise to have weekly pizza nights, whether or not the team is in town."

"Oh. I couldn't—"

He held up the screen, and her protest died on her tongue.

A picture of Brayden was there, bottom lip stuck out, pleading expression on his face.

That expression made her cave like a cheap suitcase.

"Angie's mean."

"She learned from the best." Max snorted. "But seriously," he added after she made a face at him, "I'm not going to cramp your style. Just turn up every now and again. Or preferably, more often than now and again, 'kay?"

She nodded. "Only if you let me get pineapple on the pizza."

He made a retching sound. "I'll order you your own pizza for that poison."

"Poison?"

An affronted question that had them both laughing. Then Max tugged her into another hug.

"Don't be a stranger," he murmured before giving her one more squeeze.

"I won't."

A wave and Max was gone, and Anna did not feel sad. She definitely did not feel sad.

Except, she did.

"Well, that's the story of my life," she whispered. "Isn't it?"

It was, and so she straightened her shoulders, blew out a breath, and went back into her apartment to grab her laptop.

She had colleges to apply to.

Six

BLUE

"What's up, man?" Max clapped him on the back, and Blue hurried to shove his hand back into his pocket. *Deep* into his pocket, forcing the scrap of black lace to the bottom so his teammate wouldn't know he'd held on to the piece of fabric. Or worse, that he'd found himself bringing it with him everywhere like some perverse keepsake. He didn't understand why he hadn't been able to throw out the lace after finding it under the corner of his rug a week ago, why he'd picked it up, why he'd gotten into the habit of running it between his fingertips and wishing that it was as soft as Anna's skin had been.

Well, he *didn't* know why except that perhaps he'd lost his fucking mind.

One and done had been his promise to himself.

One night and moving on.

He snorted, turning fully to face Max, giving his bud a quick, but manly hug. Because forgetting about Anna was a fucking joke. As his conscience had predicted before his dick had taken over, pretending the night with Anna hadn't happened had worked about as well as a blind backhand drop pass at the blue line.

That was to say, it didn't.

Or at least, that he hadn't been one of the rare lucky ones that actually *did* work.

"Fuck," he muttered. "I have got to get the fuck out of here."

"What was that?" Max asked, turning from where he'd been making goo-goo eyes at his fiancée, Angie, who admittedly looked gorgeous in a stunning and skimpy black dress, and so luckily, he hadn't fully heard Blue.

"Are those—?" Blue frowned, leaning closer to get a better look at Angie's dress. "Are those *droids?*"

Max grinned. "Fuck yeah, they are."

Blue's emotions tempered, the angst and frustration over his draw to Anna fading as he recognized how damned lucky his friend was. "She's perfect for you, man."

Max's expression went all soft. "Yeah," he said. "Yeah, she is."

Blue punched Max hard enough to wipe the dopey look off his face. "Get it together, bro. Yes, she's great, but fuck, at least try to pretend like you're a tough hockey player."

They were at an annual Gold fundraiser for season ticket holders. It was an evening of really good wine and food the team's nutritionist, Rebecca, wouldn't let them eat during the regular season that culminated in a live auction.

And this year, Blue had somehow ended up as the prize.

"First, Angie is a fucking goddess," Max said. "And second, I'm not the one who's agreed to be auctioned off to the highest bidder."

Truth. Despite how unfortunate it was.

Blue lifted a brow. "Have *you* ever managed to dissuade PR Rebecca from getting something she really wants?"

Two Rebeccas in the Gold organization was a lot to keep track of and so the guys had come up with a way of acknowledging who was who in any given conversation.

PR Rebecca and Nutritionist Rebecca.

Super original, albeit effective.

A knowing glint in his friend's gaze.

Max lifted his hand, palms up. "Fair point. PR Rebecca is a shark. But I still say it's a trope more along the lines of a cheesy rom-com than one belonging to a big, tough, hockey player."

Blue swung his gaze around the room, drifting it quickly past an older woman whose makeup and clothing screamed cougar, but both of which were overshadowed by the predatory look on her face. "If you'd paid attention to anything other than your gorgeous fiancée," he said. "I think you'd have given me credit for showing up at all."

"What?" Max glanced around the room and froze, as though seeing the plethora of skintight ensembles and predatory expressions for the first time. "*Oh.*"

"Yeah," Blue said. "*Oh.*"

"I think this might be the first mistake I've ever seen PR Rebecca make." He nodded at a particularly aggressive looking female. "Because that one looks like she'll tear you to shreds between the sheets."

Blue grimaced. "I mean, more power to her," he said. "She's beautiful and—" He shook his head. "I just don't think PR Rebecca and *they*"—he swept a hand in front of him, indicating the group of predatory men and women—"had the same thing in mind when she proposed the date."

Angie had come up to them as they talked. She laced her arm through Max's and smiled at Blue. "You mean PR Rebecca was imagining something more along the lines of romantic walks on the beach and not visits to *that* one's Red Room?"

Blue glanced in the direction Angie was looking.

The woman took a sip from her wineglass, making the simple act look obscene.

Max whistled. "She's going to eat you up and spit you out, Baby Blues."

Long past his annoyance with the nickname, Blue focused on the important details.

Because, fuck, both of them were right.

PR Rebecca wanted this to be a cute photo op with a reasonably attractive fan, not an X-rated film—

"Did she just do that with her tongue?" Angie whispered.

"Holy shit," Max said. "Can *you*—"

Angie smacked him.

"I think I need to talk to PR Rebecca," he said.

"I think you're right," Angie agreed.

Except as Blue moved around the room, dodging hands that seemed to have an eerie accuracy for his ass, he couldn't find Rebecca anywhere. "Fuck," he muttered, pushing through the door that led to the kitchens and hoping that she was just chewing out the caterer.

But the kitchens were empty of the stiletto-sporting, famously hard-ass publicist, and he had half a mind to just slip out the back door and remove himself from the auction block.

Except, he wouldn't do that to Rebecca.

This event was her baby, and so he would get on that stage and parade his ass around to get that high bidder, and *then* he'd go on a date. A very platonic date in a very crowded place.

Sighing, he turned and started to push back through the swinging door—

Thunk.

The *thunk* wasn't him.

Or rather it wasn't because he'd crashed into something. More like he'd shoved the door into something.

Something human.

Something female.

Something tall and slender and blond that was glaring through the porthole window at him with piercing blue eyes.

He slipped through the partially opened gap.

"Shit, Anna," he said, carefully placing himself between the door and her so she wouldn't get hit again. "Are you all right?"

Her hand came up, rubbed a spot on her right shoulder. "I'm fine."

Pale pink nails scratching up his chest, trailing down his stomach—

He blinked. "I'm sorry. I wasn't—"

"I'm fine," she said, dropping her hand to her side and stepping back. "I should go."

"Wait." He snagged her arm. "I—"

She froze, eyes on his, waiting for him to finish his sentence. Or perhaps to say something semi-articulate. Or maybe to explain why he'd left her that morning when he'd really, *really* wanted to stay.

He waited too long.

"Bye, Blue."

"Anna."

She paused but didn't turn to face him.

"I'm—"

And nothing.

He had absolutely nothing. Not one good thing to say. Except—

An announcement came over the loudspeaker, PR Rebecca declaring that the live auction would begin in five minutes.

"Bid on me," he blurted.

Blue moved around to her front, keeping his eyes deliberately on her face and not on the sexy little black dress she was wearing.

Anna frowned. "What are you talking about?"

"I'm the last auction item," he said, words coming faster now. "I promised PR Rebecca that I would go on a date, and I meant it. I didn't care if it was a man, a woman, or someone non-binary, I was happy to do it for the charity . . ."

"But?" One blond brow rose.

"But those women out there, the ones who keep making their

intentions clear with very inappropriate overtures to their wine glasses"—he shuddered—"are scary."

Her lips curved.

"I'm serious."

The curve turned into a full-blown smile. "You? Blue Anderson is afraid of a few men and women?"

"I'm terrified."

Not even a lie.

Her husky chuckle unlatched something inside him, unfroze him, had him reaching up and twining one finger around a strand of her hair. "Please, sweetheart."

Her eyes twinkled. "I don't think I have enough disposable income for the purchase of one Blue Anderson."

He tugged. "As much as I like the sound of my name on your lips, sweetheart, I don't have time to play."

"Hmm."

"Baby." He was all but begging now. "I'll reimburse you. *Please.*"

Crossed arms, cool expression, his gut sinking as several long moments passed. He stifled a sigh. She wasn't going to do it. Okay then. He just needed to deal—

"Fine."

He gaped. "What?"

Her ponytail flipped over one shoulder as she flounced away. "Get ready to make a big donation to the Gold's charity, Anderson," she called.

Fuck, he'd double it if only he got to see her walk away in that dress again.

Seven

ANNA

She felt a little bad making Blue sweat about the auction once she caught a glimpse of the crowd surrounding the stage for the live auction.

That was a lot of sexual energy.

A. Lot.

And little Blue, whose cheeks were topped with the slightest hint of an embarrassed flush, was going to get eaten alive. Anna shook her head. How a man with his skills between the sheets, who'd whispered some dirty enough things in her ear that *she'd* been the one to be blushing, was so uncomfortable in this situation was beyond her.

Confident. Hot. In absolute, total control.

That was how she would normally describe Blue.

Which meant that this glimpse of vulnerability was a dangerous, dangerous thing to her emotional well-being.

His eyes found hers in the crowd, and her breath caught. She'd always thought them such a pretty shade of blue—light, like the pale cerulean of a morning sky or the gentle cobalt of a bubbling brook or—

She was literally going insane.

How could she, Anna Hayes, possibly be writing poetry in her mind about a man's eyes?

She couldn't. She had to be hallucinating.

Because she couldn't be hung up on Blue, not when he'd left her so easily, not when he fucked anything with a vagina and two legs—hell, she wasn't even sure that the two legs were a requirement.

So, no. No poetry. No ballads or odes to his lovely eyes and his yummy dick—

But damn, what a cock.

She'd never had a man who was built like that, who knew how to use his God-given parts in ways that had so efficiently catapulted her into the heavens. Repeatedly—

Oh shit, they were bidding now.

And Anna had been off in La La Land fantasizing about how good Blue had fucked her—

"Going once," the auctioneer said.

Focus.

She raised her paddle high into the air, waving it to catch his attention.

The auctioneer nodded at her. "Twenty-five," he said. "Do I hear twenty-six?"

A woman in a tight red dress with a fur vest and sky-high heels yelled, "Thirty!"

"That had better be thirty dollars," she grumbled, narrowing her eyes up at Blue, whose panicked expression was almost priceless. Because if it was thirty thousand? People were insane. "Thirty-one."

The woman glanced over at her. Okay, she glared at Anna. "Thirty-five."

She flicked her gaze over to Blue, who was giving her a look she could only describe as please-don't-make-me-go-home-with-her. "Forty," she declared with a flick of her paddle.

"I hear forty," the auctioneer said. "Do I hear—?"

"Forty-five," the woman gritted, a sheen of sweat breaking out on her forehead.

"Fifty," Anna countered. This was kind of fun, like playing with Monopoly money.

"Fifty-five."

A wave of her paddle. "Sixty."

"Sixty-five."

Eyes back to Blue's, still reading the please-don't-stop-vibes. She was beyond hoping they were talking in tens of dollars and had moved on to praying they were talking about sixty-five *hundred* dollars—

But she'd seen an autographed jersey go for more than that during an in-game auction. This was for the live man—

Whose expression was all but begging her to not stop bidding.

Except the woman in red didn't show any signs of slowing down in her pursuit of Blue.

Still, Anna had promised.

"Seventy," she declared.

"Seventy-five," the other woman snapped, and now the sheen of sweat was on her upper lip, her cheeks flushed almost as bright as her dress. Were they finally getting to the top of her budget?

Anna decided to test that.

"Eighty-five."

The slightest dip of shoulders in response. "N-ninety."

Anna studied her closely, almost feeling bad now.

"Do I hear ninety-five?" the auctioneer asked her.

She glanced at Blue, who gave the slightest nod.

"One hundred," she said.

And, yup, Anna had broken the other woman's budget. Her shoulders sank, her paddle dropped to her side, and she shook her head at the auctioneer when he asked for "One hundred and five."

"Going once," he said. "Going twice . . ."

Anna held her breath.

"Sold."

———

The first thing she saw was Max's shocked face. The second, Angie on tiptoe, whispering furiously into his ear.

Anna had been so focused on Blue, on the woman in red and the bidding, that she'd forgotten she was in a room with more than two hundred other people. All of whom were staring at her, the silence in the room deafening.

Or maybe it was the sound of her heartbeat pounding in her ears that was drowning out the noise because the sound seemed to return in waves, whispers, soft conversations, then the normal cacophony of a party—clinking glasses, food being offered, laughter, talking—

And Blue.

Who was staring at her from the stage, eyes wide, gratitude filling their depths.

She gave him a slight nod before turning to face the person coming toward her with a clipboard in hand. The thin brown-haired man was wearing a crisp navy suit and began taking down her information while shuttling her to a table, where she was presumably going to find some way to pay an obscene amount of money.

"Sign here," the man said, and Anna glanced down at the clipboard, seeing that her fear of it being thousands and not hundreds had been well-founded.

She'd just bought Blue for one hundred thousand dollars.

Could she split it amongst like ten credit cards, she wondered, mentally calculating if she had enough credit available to get her out of this.

Maybe?

Shit.

Well, nothing to be done for it at the moment. She had to sign first, then figure it out. Hopefully Blue would pay her back before they all came due.

A hand drifted down her arm, brushed the bare skin just below the hem of her dress.

Anna jumped, jerked away. She turned and opened her mouth to tell off whatever asshole was touching her without permission. Yes, her dress was a little short, but that didn't give anyone the right to—

Oh.

Blue.

He smiled down at her, brushed the skin again, and she realized he wasn't trying to cop a feel. And no that *wasn't* disappointing. It wasn't. A stifled sigh she didn't have time for. He was trying to hand her his credit card, not touch her.

Which was fine.

It was great, actually, because she didn't have to figure out how to charge one hundred thousand dollars on her army of credit cards, and that little pang in her heart wasn't a blip of sadness. No, it was most certainly relief. Or adrenaline coming down.

Or heartburn.

Yup. She'd eaten too much cheese.

Blue smiled down at her. "Nice to meet you," he said, extending a hand. "I'm Blue."

Her brows pulled together for a heartbeat until she saw the curious expressions on the crowd surrounding them and realized this was just a show for them. She lifted her hand, placed her palm in his. "Anna."

A flash of white teeth, a smile that made her stomach tingle. "I'll be in touch, Anna," he said. "Thanks for supporting the Gold charity."

She nodded then nearly had her knees buckle when he lifted her hand to his mouth and pressed an open-mouthed kiss to her palm. One that most certainly appeared completely PG to the people around them, but also one with a flick of his wicked tongue that had her remembering exactly what that particular body part could do.

Then he was gone, and she was left with his black American Express card pressed against her heated skin.

The tepid plastic was no comparison to Blue.

EIGHT

BLUE

He skipped out of the fundraiser before any of the guys could come and either razz him or kick his ass.

Brit and Blane would tease.

Stefan, Mike, and Max would destroy.

Blue snorted, knowing that he'd been spending too much time of late with Max and Brayden and their stash of video games— *"DESTROY!"* being one of Brayden's favorite battle cries. He'd been encroaching on their father-son time, but they'd invited, and he hadn't been strong enough to say no.

Especially when he'd thought that perhaps Anna might be at their house.

No such luck.

But he'd been lucky tonight.

Less about avoiding the woman in red—because while that would have been uncomfortable, Blue knew a lot about keeping his head down and pushing through difficult situations—and more lucky because Anna cared about him enough to go to bat for him.

Or . . . maybe she didn't care and was just a good person helping someone out.

Helping family out.

Because the Gold *were* family, and Anna was a part of that.

He unlocked his car, pulled open the door, and sank into the driver's seat. It was most certainly option two—good person, helping—and not anything to do with Blue.

"You'll never amount to anything."

He froze for one long moment, shoving down the flood of pain that tore through him at the memory of that voice, trying to forget the multitude of times he'd heard that sentiment, and the fact that no matter how many times he'd heard those words, no matter how hard he'd worked to steel himself against them, that they'd still hurt.

"Perfect timing, Pops," he muttered then blew out a breath and turned on the ignition.

Blue needed to go home. He needed to sleep.

To forget tonight. To forget the past.

He needed to tuck everything back into that airtight box in his heart and mind and go back to living the life he'd crafted for himself.

Easy-breezy. Light. No drama and very little emotion.

He pulled out of the lot.

But that all could wait until tomorrow.

Because tonight he was getting drunk.

———

At first, he thought the tap-tap-tap was rain.

But even with his drink-addled brain, Blue was aware enough to know that rain in California in August just didn't happen.

He closed his eyes, took another slug of his beer, and let the sweet cacophony of *Jack Ryan* on Amazon Prime wash over him.

Ah, nothing like the sounds of explosions to help a man sleep.

Except there was that tap-tap-tap again.

He sat up. Maybe he had a leak?

Or maybe that tap-tap-tap was actually a knock-knock-knock. As in, someone was *knocking* at his front door.

"Ugh," he groaned, tossing his arm over his eyes and almost wearing his beer.

The knocking didn't stop.

"I know you're in there, idiot." Anna's voice traveled to where he sat on the couch. "The sound of shattering glass and explosions is shaking the whole damned house."

Normally a woman showing up in the middle of the night and knocking loudly on his front door would *not* be a welcome interruption.

But Blue would be lying if he said this particular woman showing up unannounced was unwelcome. Instead of hiding, he actually jumped to his feet, staggering for a second before regaining his balance, then hurried to yank open the door.

Half of him expected it to be some sort of hallucination, but it wasn't.

Anna was on his doorstep, still in that gorgeous black dress, blond hair in loose waves down her back.

"You left the party," she gritted.

He shrugged. "My part was done."

"Except"—more terseness, her jaw clenched tight—"every single person on the Gold thinks that I've been harboring some sort of insane crush on you for the past two seasons and that I've let it rot my brain to the tune of. One. Hundred. Thousand. Dollars."

Blue tried not to smile. Really, he did.

But she was just so beautiful, especially all fired up, blue eyes flashing, pink staining her cheekbones.

Of course, as with so many other things with this woman, she misinterpreted his reaction.

"Wipe that fucking smirk off your face," she snapped, pushing past him.

Heels clicking on his hardwood floor, ass swaying in that black dress—

"Eyes up here, asshole."

He'd gotten distracted by her legs, all that smooth, tanned gorgeousness, and remembering how they'd felt wrapped around his hips.

Blue's gaze whipped to hers. "Hi, beautiful."

Her lips pressed into a flat line, and he couldn't stop himself from closing the distance between them, from brushing his thumb across the bottom one. "Don't," he murmured. "Don't do that."

Her mouth parted slightly, a little puff of moist air escaping to glaze the pad of his finger.

"Do what?" she asked.

"Hurt these lush lips."

A sniff. "You're drunk."

He shrugged, turned back to the couch, crossing over to plunk down onto it. "So?"

Silence.

He flicked his stare over to her, feeling less buzzed by the moment.

Well, less drunk on alcohol and more drunk on Anna.

God, she was pretty and smart and . . . called him out on his shit. Only two of those things were characteristics he'd thought he wanted in a woman. But with Anna, that trifecta was only the beginning of all the things he liked about her. She was loyal and funny, kind and freakishly organized. He desperately wanted that other night to have been the start of something . . .

And he just didn't know how.

Not when his plan was—

Fuck your plan.

There it was.

Such a simple fucking answer and—

Anna dropped his credit card on the coffee table. "All paid up. No need to redeem that date." She hesitated for a heartbeat before sighing. "Well, *you're welcome*, I guess."

A click of her heels as she spun toward the door.

"Wait." Blue was on his feet before he realized he'd moved. "I'm sorry," he said. "I'm screwing this all up. I—" He shook his head. "I'm not supposed to like you."

"Wow." Her laugh was brittle. "Thanks, I guess?"

"No," he said, taking her hand. "That's not what I mean. I-I had this picture in my head of the woman I wanted to be with. Sweet and kind and . . . calm, I guess. You're not those things—"

She pulled back.

"You're tough and abrupt and don't care that you don't have a lot of friends. You're independent and never hesitate to call people on their shit—"

"I think I've heard enough," she said softly.

"Anna, I'm trying to tell you that it's good you're the way you are."

A heartbeat of silence before a shadow crossed her eyes. "Sure, you are." She dodged him when he would have snagged her arm. "Bye, Blue."

"Wait."

She didn't.

And he didn't go after her.

Fucking pathetic coward.

NINE

A ugust and September passed in a blur.

Anna had signed up for a full load of classes at the local community college, knowing she needed to get back into the swing of school and homework and—giant *ugh* coming—Blue Books and Scantrons.

Most of her waking moments had been full to the brim—the mornings with classes, the evenings with math problems she hadn't seen in years and reading and so many essays that she thought she'd go crazy—but she had managed to both squeeze in some free time to spend with Brayden, Max, and Angie and also applied to several of the local four-year colleges for their winter trimester.

And now she had returned from classes to a full mailbox, on top of which was an envelope from her top choice.

One she'd been staring at for a solid two minutes.

A *normal*-sized envelope.

Wasn't it supposed to be bigger?

She snorted, tucking it into her bag before taking the two flights of stairs up to her apartment. That's what they all said.

Oh well, it was probably too much for her to actually expect to have gotten in on an odd trimester after a long break from school on her first try. She'd stick with community college for a bit, knock off some of those general ed requirements.

By the time she was unlocking the door to her apartment, she was slightly out of breath and sweating.

Textbooks were heavy.

Who knew?

Another snort.

And apparently, she was turning into a snort monster.

Lame, but Brayden would have laughed.

"Come on, Anna," she murmured, extracting her keys and pushing in through her front door, her heart heavy from missing Brayden. "Get it together."

Bray was well adjusted and happy, excited to be his dad's best man in the upcoming wedding.

Anna had teased Max and Angie about jumping the gun into marriage, but she couldn't exactly fault their logic. A wedding during the season would be tough. It would have to be crammed into a non-game night, and a honeymoon would be hard to pull off.

So it was either do it now, before the season really got going with a short honeymoon, or wait until the end of the season.

But even waiting was hard to schedule with playoffs going for who knew how long and teammates traveling home for the summer break. The wedding would be easier to host when everyone the happy couple wanted to attend would be close by.

Her phone buzzed just as she'd set down her heavy backpack and turned back to throw the dead bolt.

She pulled it out of her pocket and smiled.

Brayden had recently gotten one of those phones where he could text three people and Anna was one of the three.

Gold star for her.

Or maybe that would convince Blue she did actually have friends, even if they were only nine.

"You don't care that you don't have a lot of friends."

Yeah, that one stung.

Look, she got it. She could come off rough and sometimes she said stuff without a polite sugarcoating, but that didn't mean she didn't care about other people, that she didn't feel. She loved and hurt and cried at *Grey's Anatomy*, just like everyone else.

She just had a few more walls in place to protect her when those she cared about left her or died or cut her off.

Because people didn't really stick.

Not for a lifetime . . . or at least not with *her* they didn't.

Her own parents had left one day then never returned. No one knew if they were alive or dead and, frankly, Anna had stopped caring about either outcome a long time ago.

Or tried to anyway.

Because it hurt.

Being abandoned hurt. Fancy that.

And . . . sarcasm to cure bone-deep hurts for the win.

Anyway, her grandmother had taken her in at first, but hadn't been able to care for her for long—she'd been ill with a progressive neurological disorder for years—and so Anna had been shuttled between aunts and cousins during her grandma's ever-increasing hospital stays.

And when her grandmother had died, Anna had ended up in a group home.

Nine years old.

Alone.

And so now she'd had twenty years on her own.

She hadn't been one of the lucky ones. There hadn't been a fairy tale ending, no fantastic foster parents to rescue her—though she was grateful for the ones who were out there for other kids. Her situation just hadn't been that.

Clothes in a black garbage bag, meals sometimes few and far between, dirty hair and itchy skin from running out of shampoo or from having to use it as body wash. Noise and crying and kids turning on each other.

She'd been one of the lucky ones, had turned eighteen after high school graduation and had been able to earn her diploma before being forced out of the system.

But she hadn't been able to afford college without working full-time and between tuition, books, rent, and food the couple of scholarships she'd qualified for hadn't given her enough to live on. Which meant her progress on her degree had been minuscule.

Eventually, she'd dropped out, taking care of a neighbor who'd fallen ill for a few months, who'd then referred her to a friend who had happened to be Stefan Barie's mother.

The Gold captain had been here in California when his mother had fallen ill back in Minnesota, and luck had been on Anna's side because she'd only been in the next town over, renting a shitty apartment with her lease up the subsequent month.

She'd moved in with Diane, had driven her to her doctor's appointments, held her hand when she'd been sick from chemo, had prayed and wished and hoped she would recover.

Diane *had* recovered.

She'd also moved to California, left the cold and snow and humidity behind.

And Anna. She'd also been left behind.

Which wasn't a fair thought because Anna wasn't Diane's responsibility. She was an employee, plain and simple. Plus, it wasn't like they'd forgotten about her. When Max had needed help with Brayden, Stefan had recommended her.

And taking care of Brayden had been the best thing she'd ever done with her life.

So yeah, she was thrilled to be in Bray's top three.

Anna? Did you not like my meme?

She blinked, still holding her cell, and focused on the little boy's messages.

Dude. It's hilarious. I was just searching for one that was just as funny.

Quickly, she scoured her phone for a GIF that was sure to make him laugh. Which wasn't all that hard, especially because he loved dogs and was thoroughly entertained by butts, farts, and any joke pertaining to either of those.

A corgi with sunglasses on his butt. Perfect. Sold. She sent it and awaited his response.

Not to be outdone, he replied back with a pug wearing sunglasses that read, "Stay Cool."

Chuckling, she shook her head and pressed the call button on her cell.

"'Lo?" Bray answered a few seconds later.

"At much as I love texting with you," she said. "I wanted to hear your voice. How did your book report go?"

"Fine. Guess what?"

"What?"

"I was playing Minecraft with Marcus and we made a house and filled it with like a hundred creepers and then he accidentally made it explode. It was crazy. We tried to run but . . ."

Anna was well versed in Minecraft and so was able to translate that.

"Then what happened?"

"We respawned and then lost all of our armor, but guess what?"

She smiled. "What?"

"I found mine!"

"That's great, bud," she said. "Everything else going okay? You still like your teacher?"

"Yup."

"And soccer?"

"Yup."

"Gonna play hockey this season?"

"Nope."

Anna froze. "What's your dad say about that?"

Bray sighed. "He says I should do what makes me happy, so long as one of those things isn't just video games." A beat. "I need to not forget to exercise."

"I think you get plenty of that," she said.

"Yup. That's what Dad said." He paused, and she could almost sense the words struggling to fruition in his brain. "Something about habits or health or . . ."

"Healthy habits?"

"Yes! That video games are fine, but my body needs exercise to work. Just like how you can't make an Iron Gollum without—"

And here she lost her battle with Minecraft terms.

Or at least her brain glazed over.

"Oh!" Brayden suddenly exclaimed. "Angie and I are making cookies. She says I need to add the chocolate chips!"

"Fun," Anna said. "Love you. Bye"

"Love you. Bye," he said back, though so quickly that it might as well have been one word.

Smiling, she tucked her phone back into her pocket and settled down at her dining room table.

The little envelope stared back at her.

"Fuck it," she muttered and tore open the flap.

Then gaped.

Because apparently little *could* mean good.

Especially in this case, as she'd been accepted into the program. Come January, she would officially be on her way to becoming a teacher.

Anna sat there for a long moment, the paper crushed against her chest.

Her smile was so big it hurt her cheeks.

Carefully, she folded it and set it next to her laptop then settled in to work. She'd swung for the fences, and for once in her life, the ball had actually made it over.

Home run.

And so now she needed to not screw it up.

Step one of that? She had homework to crush.

TEN

BLUE

He'd fucked up.

He should have come up with an excuse to miss Max's wedding. Faked being sick—was the bird flu still a thing?—or made up a death in the family.

Except, Max knew that Blue didn't have any family.

His parents had passed a couple of years before and as an only child and a military brat to boot, connections tended to be few and far between.

Just the guys.

Or well, the guys *and* girls.

Because aside from Brit being his teammate and friend, he'd become close with his friends' wives—with Sara, Angie, Mandy, and Monique, their former goalie, Spence's, wife.

"You just like hanging with them because they mother you," Anna had teased a few months back.

If she'd only known how right she was.

Blue had been short on mothering for a long time.

His own mother had been in the military, his father the stay-at-home parent.

Which had basically meant that he'd had year-long stints of TV dinners and signing his own permission slips, punctuated by visits home from a mom who cared deeply but who also just didn't have much of a mothering instinct.

She was never the mom to make cookies for the school bake sale or to make sure he had new clothes for back to school or to write encouraging notes and stick them in his lunch box.

Blue had made his own lunch.

Or it hadn't gotten made.

He sighed and tugged at his tie, watching the guests starting to file into their seats, all while knowing he couldn't hold it against his parents too much. He'd had food, a safe place to stay, he'd gotten rides to school and hockey practice—the first because school was required by law and the second because hockey was one extracurricular that his dad was all in on.

Bruins fan for life.

Blue bit back a smile.

He knew he was lucky in so many ways.

It just would have been nice to know that he'd been loved, that he hadn't been some unplanned burden, especially since that was how he'd felt for most of his life.

Unwanted. An unnecessary complication and—

Fuck.

This was getting really heavy for a wedding.

"You need to take Anna on that date."

He jumped, no way to play it off, not when PR Rebecca somehow managed to sneak up on him in five-inch stilettos.

Off his game.

Yeah, since his Anna-induced orgasm haze.

No.

Blue stifled a sigh because he wasn't off his game due to

orgasms—or a lack thereof, if he was being totally honest. He hadn't been able to sleep with anyone since that night with Anna, and though he'd been trying to convince himself that his dick was just tired of playing the field—read, he'd had such a long enough streak of pussy that it just couldn't be bothered—Blue knew it wasn't that he'd finally gotten his fill of women. Nope, it was because he'd finally gotten his fill of women who *weren't* Anna.

And also because he'd hurt her.

Just the reminder of that slice of pain sliding across her face, the way her bright blue eyes had dimmed, made him feel like the world's biggest asshole all over again.

"Anna doesn't like me," he said, focusing on the problem in front of him.

The problem he could fix.

Leaving Anna alone so he didn't hurt her again.

"She spent a hundred thousand dollars on you," Rebecca said. "If she doesn't like you then at least she wants to fu—"

Cutting her off before she got too close to the truth, Blue shook his head. "Did you even look at the name on the card before you charged it?"

PR Rebecca froze, brows furrowing for a split second. "Blue Anderson!"

He shot her a chagrined smile. "Those bidders were scary."

"You—" Brightly painted red lips parted before she sighed, her tone softening, almost musing. "You're right. That woman in red might have given me a story I couldn't spin." Her eyes shot to his, narrowed. "Don't think I'm refunding you that money."

Blue lifted his hands in surrender. "No," he said. "I just considered it a donation."

"Hmm." The glared stayed in place long enough for him to really start to sweat. "You still need to give me a date."

He shook his head again. "Remember the whole *Anna doesn't like me* thing?"

"Easy to see why—"

"Hey!"

"Shush you. I don't care if she likes you or not," Rebecca said. "I need social media fodder and, my dear, you promised me a date with pictures."

Blue's mouth dropped open. "First of all, you guilted me into that date, and second of all, you threw me to the wolves. Those women—"

"And men," Rebecca interjected with a shark-like smile.

He narrowed his eyes but amended. "And men. I don't care about gender so much as I care about what they had planned for me." He lifted a palm when she opened her mouth again. "Don't prevaricate. Whatever it was, you know it wasn't a nice dinner followed by a movie."

A beat. "No," she eventually said. "I did do some research on the woman in red after that night. Turns out that she moonlights as a dominatrix. Which is great. I'm all for us girls to go after what we want"—Rebecca made a face—"Although I'd prefer for her X-rated activities to not be attached to my family-friendly hockey team."

"See?" Blue said. "I did you a favor *and* gave you a giant donation. My work here is done."

Rebecca glared. "You played the system."

He sighed. "I thought we just agreed that was a good thing." He pointed around them. "Plus, if you want social media fodder, wouldn't a *wedding* be a much better catch?"

Silence. The glare turning into a deadly expression that Blue had no problem admitting scared him.

"A wedding is a sacred event," Rebecca snapped. "It is Max and Angie's special day, and I won't ruin it with attention they don't want."

A slender blonde tossed her arm around Rebecca's shoulder. "Wow," Brit said. "I think that is the most human thing I've ever heard you say." She stepped to the side, nudged Rebecca's arm. "What have you done with our publicist?"

"Shut up," Rebecca grumbled. "It's important."

"Yes, it is," Brit agreed. "So underneath all those designer dresses and spiked heels, you're a big softy."

She shoved her finger in their faces in turn. "Don't. Tell anyone."

"We won't," they echoed.

"And you'll go on that date?" she asked, eyes locked with his.

"What? No. I didn't say—"

Brit smacked him. "He'll go. Anna deserves a night out. She's been busting her ass helping with the wedding and going to classes."

"I—"

It was Brit's turn to glare at him. "Did you know that she made all of the flower arrangements?" He shook his head. "Well, she did because the florist broke her leg two days ago, and so Anna stepped in. And the decorations? Want to guess who did those when the wedding coordinator was dealing with the caterers? Hmm?"

"Anna."

Brit threw up her hands. "Of course, Anna," she said. "And so she deserves a nice night out. One with a guy who can be charming and not take advantage."

The last words were a warning.

"I'm not saying she doesn't deserve a night out," he said. "But wouldn't it be better with someone who she actually likes?"

Brit's mouth curved. "Probably."

A shrug from Rebecca. "But since there's not one of them around, you'll do."

Wow.

"And here I'd thought you guys had my back."

Brit snorted. "We do," she said. "But we also have Anna's, and I know she needs a couple of hours break and some food that isn't from a college cafeteria."

Rebecca nodded. "Exactly. Treat Anna and snap one selfie. That's all I'm asking."

"Rebecca!" Brit said, realization suddenly dawning on her face. "Is that what this is about? PR nonsense?"

A shrug that was devoid of guilt. "It's not nonsense."

Brit put on her scary face. "Dinner for Anna. But only because she's with Max and Angie and Brayden. Oh, and because she's awesome."

Rebecca's bright fire-engine red lips parted.

"And no freaking selfies," Brit declared. "The Gold doesn't take advantage of their players that way."

Though the "not *anymore*" wasn't spoken, it was still there.

Brit and Stefan had eloped, but their road to marriage hadn't been straight. Their relationship had begun as a publicity stunt concocted by the previous management, and while the end product was good because Stefan and Brit were happy, neither of them had been on board with the process.

The publicist pouted. "Fine."

Brit bumped her shoulder against Rebecca's. "Maybe they'll end up like Stefan and me, and this will be a really good story for *Gold Time*."

Blue groaned as Rebecca's grin widened. "Oh, yes," she said. "I can see it now. *Love Found on the Auction Block*"—she winced— "No, that's tone-deaf. Maybe *Bidding for Love?*"

"Better," Brit agreed. "Or—*oh!* How about *Saved by the Gavel?*"

"Holy fucking shit," he muttered. "I've entered an alternate universe. I'll take Anna out on a date because you asked and it sounds like she needs a distraction, but no selfies, no fucking love features on *Gold Time*. That woman is the last person I can imagine falling for. She's just—"

Brit socked him. Hard.

Right in the kidney.

And he knew. Even before he turned and saw Anna standing behind him, hurt staining her features because of him. Again.

Son of a bitch.

He'd fucked up.

Again.

ELEVEN

ANNA

Wow.

Why did she keep doing this to herself?

Why did she keep allowing Blue's words to hurt her?

Normally she was a fucking steel wall. Never let anyone too close and if someone *did* happen to somehow make it past any of her barriers, they'd proven to her over and over and *over* again that they could be trusted.

Five people.

As in, that was the number of people who'd weaseled their way into Anna's heart.

Brayden, Diane, Max, Angie, and Stefan.

Well, six.

Because Brit made Stefan happy and loved Diane as much as Anna did . . . and maybe also because she'd been nice to Anna, not pushing her to connect, but always helping her to feel included.

But the point was that Blue wasn't part of that six. He was just a guy she'd slept with once—

Cough.

Okay, four times.

Still, it had only been one night, so she shouldn't be vulnerable to him, and he *definitely* shouldn't be able to get to her, to hurt her, to make her feel like shit.

Too bad he did anyway.

Well, no more.

She set down the spool of ribbon she'd been stringing through the final row of chairs and pulled out her cell from the pocket of her dress—yes, her dress had pockets and yes, it was amazeballs for mostly that reason . . . and also because it made her body look amazing.

In this moment, she was exceptionally glad for that small fact.

Stepping into Blue's arms was too easy, too comfortable, too—

She rose up on tiptoe and pressed her mouth to his cheek.

Click.

Anna forced a smile as she stepped back. "There's your date," she told Rebecca. "Put your PR skills to work."

"Anna—" Brit began.

"Will you forward that over to Rebecca?" she asked Brit. "I don't have her number."

"I—"

"Great. Thanks." She pocketed her cell then bent, snatched up the ribbon, and made her escape, bee-lining straight for the bathroom.

Thank God it was a single stall.

She slammed and locked the door, leaning back against it and trying to breathe.

Untouchable.

That was supposed to be her.

Unfeeling.

God, it had been so much better when she'd been unfeeling. This? Hurting because an idiotic man managed to poke a particularly open wound? This really fucking sucked.

Eyes burning, she turned for the sink.

"Ugh," she muttered, wetting a paper towel and dabbing at the corners of her eyes. "No more. This is a happy day."

That reminder was enough for Anna to suck in a deep breath, to shove away her hurt feelings, and to focus on what was important: Brayden, Angie, and Max.

Ribbons. Flowers. The ceremony.

Hoping to God that the wedding planner and the caterer had managed to repair the toppled cake.

Yup. *Those* were the things she needed to concentrate on.

Not Blue Fucking Anderson or his barbed insults.

Or his pretty eyes. Or sexy words.

Or that way he'd made her feel that night.

Because *none* of it made up for how he'd made her feel in that moment.

———

Angie made an absolutely gorgeous bride.

Her dress was the lightest shade of periwinkle, with crystals dotted sporadically on the lace overlay. But it was the rest of her appearance that was so Angie—her hair curled and styled half-up, half-down, a crystal droid securing the intricate coiffure, the matching R2-D2 pumps peeking from beneath her hem.

Nerds.

The both of them.

And absolutely perfect for one another.

"You look beautiful," she whispered as she hugged the bride tight.

"Thank you," Angie murmured, blush creeping into her cheeks. "I— This—" She shook her head.

"It's a lot," Anna supplied. "But you guys deserve it. Hush, you," she added when Angie shook her head again and opened her mouth, presumably to argue. "You deserve your happy ending, you and Max *and* Brayden."

Angie blinked. "Damn you!" she exclaimed. "How did I get so lucky to have you all in my life? So . . . just *damn you.*"

Anna grinned, blinking herself. "Damn, yourself," she teased, squeezing Angie one more time. "Thank you," she whispered. "For making them happy."

Angie kissed her cheek. "You make us happy, too. Don't forget that, okay?"

A nod. "Okay."

"Good. Now"—a wide smile spread the other woman's lips— "I get to go dance with my husband."

Anna's own lips were curved as she watched Angie drag Max onto the dance floor. At least they were before she turned around and saw who was standing behind her.

"Can we talk, sweetheart?" Blue asked, voice almost gentle.

Her heart skipped a beat at the endearment before she could lock it down. *Get it together, Hayes.* Ignore the charm. Stifle the feelings. Move it right along. "I think we've *talked* enough." She brushed by him. "And I'm not your fucking *sweetheart,* so just leave me alone, Blue."

There, she thought since he didn't try to stop her from walking away. *It's done.*

Peace was what she felt in that moment. Definitely. Just relief that she could tuck away the anomaly of Blue and all the feelings he brought along with him. Not disappointment that things couldn't be different.

But, dammit, she had too much self-respect to continue feeling like this every time they met.

Everything was fine when she didn't see him, but that wasn't reality. Their social circles overlapped and so, if she wanted to see Brayden and Max, Angie, Brit, and Diane, if she wanted to talk to Stefan, there would always be the chance of Blue being somewhere in the picture.

She needed to deal or let them all go.

And since she couldn't let go of the little family she'd begun to call her own, her only option was to shut up and deal.

Just not tonight.

Tonight, she'd had enough. Her feet were screaming, and the dress that had been bordering on too tight at the beginning of the afternoon was now one slice of cake away from bursting at the seams.

She bent to straighten a flower and felt the stitches all but groan in protest.

So maybe less than a slice of cake away.

But that was okay. Her job here was done. The cake in question—now repaired and a three-tier homage to nerdiness—had been sliced and distributed. Drinks were flowing, and the DJ was playing a nice selection of music. Young enough to be popular but still easy to dance to.

No one would even notice if she slipped out.

Plus, she had an essay due on Monday and really needed to—

Make an excuse to GTFO.

Whatever. The point was she'd been there long enough, so she was going home to her textbooks and laptop and bottle of rum punch, and no one would care. Nodding, she tucked her purse under one arm then went and retrieved her coat from the check stand. It was only once she'd made it into the parking lot that she realized the problem with leaving early.

Because the venue had limited spaces and Stefan and Brit had picked her up.

Le. Sigh.

Über it was.

Anna swiped at the screen of her cell, unlocking it and opening the app, but before she could finish the request, calloused fingers brushed the bare skin on her shoulder.

"Can I give you a ride?"

Blue. Because *of course* it was Blue.

"No," she said coldly. "I'm fine."

He came around to face her, crouching a bit so he could meet her eyes. "I always say the wrong thing when I'm around you." A slight curve at the corner of his mouth. "You know how alcohol sometimes makes people lose their filter? Well, you're my alcohol."

"Is your argument that I make you say stupid shit?" She sniffed. "Because case in point, I haven't done anything to you, Blue."

"Yes, you have," he said quietly, straightening and pulling out the key fob to his car and pressing a button. The lights on the sedan in front of them flashed. "But it's not your fault. I'm the asshole here."

A snort was her only response.

"Since we're both in agreement with that, why don't you let me give you a lift home? It's the least I can do."

"No." Anna pressed a button on her phone then felt obligated to add, "Thanks."

Silence.

She glanced up, despite knowing that Blue was still standing in front of her, still watching her closely.

"I'm fine."

"Chicken?"

Her breath caught. He was so not—

"Buck-buck-*buuuck*."

He was. The fucking bastard.

She crossed her arms. "I'm not going home with you."

"I'm not asking you to." He walked over to his car, tugged open the passenger side door. "I'm just offering you a ride . . . and maybe an explanation."

"I think you've said enough already."

"Please, Anna?"

She didn't move.

"Please?" he asked again. "I promise to not say anything stupid."

She lifted a brow.

"Okay"—he chuckled—"how about I promise to *try* and not say something stupid?"

Chin dropping to her chest with a sigh, Anna considered her options. On the one hand, she never wanted to deal with him again. On the other, she'd just been psyching herself up because she knew she would most certainly have to interact with Blue on a —if not regular—then at least on a semi-regular basis.

"You can call me names," he cajoled. "I'll even help you think of some really good ones."

Her laugh escaped despite best efforts.

Too damned charming for his own good.

"Fine," she said with a sigh. "You can drive me home."

His smile took her breath away, and she didn't get it back as he snagged her elbow and tucked her into the passenger seat of his car. It stayed gone as he reached over to snap in her seat belt and continued its vacation as he straightened a lock of her hair.

Only the jolt of the car door slamming had her sucking in a deep lungful of air.

But then he was right back next to her, belt clicking, door locks engaging, and . . . her mind lost track of anything except his spicy scent filling the space between them, the way his arm brushing hers sent a spark through her insides, reminding her all over again how good that night had been.

He turned to face her fully, indigo eyes intense enough to have her lungs considering a second hiatus.

"I am so sorry," he said, words bursting out of him so quickly Anna had a hard time following at first. "I had this plan. One that was supposed to make my life finally feel full, but now I see how fucking stupid it was." A shake of his head. "I just thought that if I followed the plan, if I found someone like my friends did, then I would be happy. Like they are. But I'm not them."

"Um, no?"

He plunked his head onto his steering wheel. "I'm majorly fucking this up."

"Yes, you are."

His gaze shot to hers in surprise, a heartbeat passing before he realized she was teasing, and his smile matched the one she could feel curving her lips.

"I didn't mean those things I was saying as an insult."

"Blue." She gave him a look. "They weren't good."

His expression went a touch chagrined. "I—"

"Just drive, okay?" she said. "Let's pause this conversation before another one of those not-insults lands true."

He studied her for a long moment then sighed and nodded. He put the car into drive and backed from the spot. "I'm yours to direct."

TWELVE

BLUE

He waited until they were on the freeway before saying anything else.

"Can I at least explain?"

A sigh. "I thought we were doing away with any extraneous words."

"Well," he said, amusement slicing through him at the terse words. "I just figured that since I've got you trapped, I might as well try to explain."

"Trapped?" She groaned and pretended to reach for the door handle. "Not if I tuck and roll."

"Hilarious," he said, making sure the locks were engaged, but he was smiling because she was too damned funny for her own good. "Please avoid the tucking and rolling."

"If you insist." But then her tone went serious. "Blue, I'm not a glutton for punishment, and I'm definitely not a punching bag anymore. However our night together ended, I still deserve to be treated with kindness and respect."

His hands tightened on the steering wheel, filing the word

anymore away to ponder later, because that single insight into Anna's past made him realize how little he knew about her, aside from the fact that she'd grown up in Minnesota and had taken care of Stefan's mom and then Brayden.

Not a punching bag. Anymore.

Well, he'd done a damned good job of making her feel like one, huh?

"Shit, sweetheart. I—" He sighed then just decided to level with her. "My parents didn't want me."

She froze, glanced over at him.

He felt it, even though he kept his eyes determinedly on the road.

"I'm sure they—"

He met her stare for one brief moment. "No," he said. "They'd chosen to not have kids, and I was the unwelcome surprise." A beat. "A direct quote, though one I don't think I was supposed to actually hear."

His parents hadn't been cruel, just unattached and minimally interested.

His mom had been deployed multiple times during his child-hood, and then when she'd retired from active duty, had spent more months out of the country than in it for her civilian job.

"I—uh—"

"They were both in the military, and I messed that up. Or at least for my dad." He signaled and pulled into the next lane. "My mom had the better assignment, so my dad retired when his discharge came up. The trouble was that he didn't want to be a stay-at-home parent. He wanted to be in the military."

"They shouldn't have had a kid then," Anna said softly.

"Agreed." But he added, because it was another unfortunate truth he'd learned as a ten-year-old boy who'd accidentally eaves-dropped on a conversation that he never should have heard, "That's why my father had a vasectomy."

"Oh."

"Yeah." A sigh as he exited the freeway at the off-ramp Anna indicated. "And apparently my mom was also on birth control to control irregular periods. *Barf.*"

Her eyes were soft. "Seriously."

"Apparently, I was determined to be born."

The barest smile at his wry words. "That determination is probably why you're such a good hockey player."

"No." He shook his head. "I'm good at hockey because it was the only thing my dad took interest in."

Her breath caught, silence reigning over the car.

"Fuck, Blue," she said. "You had to pull out the big guns, didn't you?"

Amusement swelled, bubbling over as he burst out laughing over something that had never been funny before. It still wasn't, he supposed, but somehow that simple teasing from Anna had made him feel lighter.

"I just want you to understand where I was coming from. My entire childhood was me making plans and contingencies, trying to find a way for my parents to love me. If I only got straight A's or made a certain team or was independent enough so they didn't have to bother with me, then maybe . . ."

"Things would change?"

"Yeah." He shrugged. "They didn't, of course, and eventually I came to realize that the one person I could count on was me. I never planned on being in a relationship with anyone."

"Hence the string of women through your bedroom?"

He nodded. "Easier to feel good without getting attached," he said. "But the truth was that while it was really exciting at first, that lack of connection got old fast, especially when I saw the guys and Brit finding someone they could be really happy with, and I—fuck this makes me sound like the biggest pussy on the planet—but I wanted to be like them."

"Turn here," she said, pointing up at the next street. "And what's that old saying? Pussy is the toughest thing around because it takes a pounding?" She smirked when he snorted. "My point is that it's not weak to want to be loved."

"Yeah."

"So, you decided to hang up your bachelor shoes?"

"Something like that."

"It's hard to look at them all sickeningly happy and not want that."

"That's true."

"Fuckers."

Blue's heart squeezed at her light tone. "Every one of them."

She snorted. "Here's my building." He found an empty spot and pulled to the curb, waiting as she gathered up her purse and coat. "I'm guessing," she said as she paused, fingers on the handle. "That I'm not the type of woman you'd planned on."

"No," he agreed.

A shadow in her expression before she forced a smile that made his teeth ache it was so sugary and fake. "Well, at least you're off the hook for that date now."

"You're not the type of woman I ever pictured myself with—"

"Oh, please stop showering me with flowery, affectionate words." Both hands came up, palms out. "I get it. I'll leave you to your perfect, sweet future girlfriend."

Leaning over the console, fingers on her arm, movement before Blue consciously thought about it.

"No," he repeated. "You're not the type of woman I imagined I would be with."

She shrugged him off. "Yeah. Got that."

"Anna." He cupped her cheek. "You're so much more."

Her response was shaky, a slow movement that had his palm sliding off her face. "You don't even know me." She popped the door handle.

"I'd like to," he said softly, trying not to scare her off, not when he finally understood all the twisted feelings inside his heart. No,

Anna hadn't been in his plan. No, she wasn't what he'd expected. But maybe . . . maybe she was better.

She shook her head, almost violently, and pushed open the door. "I-I can't."

He shoved open his own door, rounding the front of his car. "Wait. *Anna*."

He grabbed her arm, stopping her when she would have bolted away.

Her expression sliced him to the quick—hurt and fear. No, not merely fear. It was terror. He'd terrified her.

"I can't, Blue. I-I just can't do this."

"I understand." He squeezed her arm gently then stepped back, releasing her. "You don't have to, sweetheart."

"Of course, I don't," she said, steady now as she lifted her chin and fiddled with the strap of her purse.

"I'm so sorry I hurt you," he blurted. "But I'm also really sorry that someone else did, too."

Another one of those almost violent movements, this time a nod. But she didn't say anything else as she turned toward her building.

"Bye, Anna," he murmured.

"Goodbye, Blue."

Then she was gone.

And his heart ached at the very thought.

THIRTEEN

ANNA

The text came two days later.

So, I know I blew my chance and I promised not to bug you, but this made me think of you.

A second buzz followed a heartbeat after, and she smiled at the picture of a shirt emblazoned with, "You don't scare me. I successfully negotiate with kids for a living."

Aw.

Blue had left her alone, well for two days at least, but just because he hadn't been there in body didn't mean he was out of her thoughts. If she were being truthful, she would have said that she'd thought of little else aside from Blue and what he'd told her over the last forty-eight hours.

So much clarity.

So much sympathy.

And yet, did any of it really make a lick of difference?

"No," she said, pushing the textbook on child development to the side and flopping onto her back on her couch. "Yes."

Because she got it.

She understood what it was like to feel unwanted and that defense mechanisms often came along with a childhood like hers or Blue's. She also knew what it was like to weigh the decision to let someone in very carefully, after having been burned and hurt over and *over* again.

But—and it was a big but—did knowing why he'd reacted the way he did make any bit of difference?

Because in the end, it was *her* heart and emotional well-being on the line.

And yet, did all of the protecting of her heart and her emotions and herself above all else change anything?

No, because she could think of *nothing* but Blue.

Blue focused on her that night.

Blue's words that had stung so readily.

Blue in the car, earnest and open.

"Fuck," she muttered and just gave in.

Where are you?

A few seconds before:

The pier. Getting my sea lion fix.

A video of the sea lions that lived behind the pier appeared on her cell and had her in hysterics as she watched them bark and jostle for position while one very determined pup vied for position at the top of the pile.

Another buzz, another message from Blue.

Where are you?

As she hesitated, debating a response, her phone vibrated again.

Never mind. I promised to leave you alone and now I'm pestering you again. I'm sorry.

Anna's fingertips tapped the side of her cell, still unsure, still going around that mental merry-go-round.

I love the pier.

Four words and yet the way her heart pounded after sending them, the shuddering breath she released after pressing that blue and white button, and you would have thought she'd just submitted a four-hundred-page novel that had been her life's work.

What's your favorite part?

Her shoulders relaxed.

There's this crab shop at Pier 41, slightly off the tourist trap, but they have the best clam chowder in the world.

His response made them hunch right back up.

Want to come and have some with me?

She bit her lip, mostly scared because she wanted to do exactly that. She *wanted* to hang out on the pier and have dessert first, maybe some ice cream, maybe some fudge, and then she wanted to go have a giant sourdough bread bowl filled with clam chowder. It made no sense—not the food part because *yum*—but why she would want to put herself out there with him after being burned.

And yet, Anna couldn't deny that she'd felt drawn to Blue from the moment he'd tried to pick her up outside the arena.

The memory made her smile, propelled her fingers into motion.

Will you use another horrible pick up line on me if I do?

A buzz.

Are you French?

She frowned.

Um. No.

His response made her chuckle.

Because Eiffel for you.

Oh my God. That's awful.

There's more where that came from.

She shook her head, blew out a breath, and sent:

You buy me cookie-dough fudge and I'll get the clam chowder.

Blue's response came in just a second.

You have yourself a deal. Thirty minutes give you enough time?

Absolutely.

Anna tossed her phone onto the couch cushion then froze for one long moment, her heart thudding, her hands over her face.

"I can't believe you just did that." A groaning response to herself, but she was smiling, and if she'd actually acknowledged the floating feeling in her heart, she would have said that she was excited.

And hopeful.

And . . . really freaking underdressed.

"Shit!"

Anna jumped up and spun in a useless circle. She was wearing her oldest pajamas and even qualifying them as clothing was a stretch. The fabric was so thin near the seams that one wrong move would bring about their end. Not to mention the fact that she couldn't answer the door without putting on her robe, or else risk an arrest for public nudity.

She rolled her eyes at herself.

Yes, she was being dramatic.

But it was better to focus on a peep show and not the fact that she was meeting Blue.

Oh shit.

She had—she risked a peek at her cell—twenty-six minutes until she was supposed to meet Blue at the pier, and it was at least a twenty-minute Über ride.

What had she been thinking?

Not about how long it would take to make herself presentable, that was for sure.

Well, nothing to be done for it. She requested the ride before running for her bedroom.

Anna tore off her tank top and pants, letting them fall to the floor, then scrambled for a pair of jeans and a shirt that wouldn't get her arrested. One minute to brush her tangled mat of hair and yank it up into a ponytail and another to slap on some mascara and lip gloss. A hurried grab for her purse, quickly locking up, before bolting down the stairs. She pushed out the front door of her building the same moment the car pulled up.

"Hi," she said, breathless as she hopped into the back.

"How's it going?" the driver asked and then didn't give her a second to answer before proceeding to chat her ear off about his cousin's niece's daughter's dance competition and how she was going to be featured on a new reality show for up-and-coming dancers.

Normally, the sheer volume of conversation would have driven her nuts—she preferred to scroll through her phone with the bare minimum of talking on her rides—but in this case, her driver was perfect.

She was ridiculously nervous, her palms sweaty, her heart pounding, and all but ready to test those "tuck and roll" skills she'd teased Blue about.

So the distraction was welcome.

And the twenty-minute drive felt like seconds.

"Here you are," he said, pulling up to the curb. "You have a fun time."

"Thanks." She opened the door and pushed out, realizing that she hadn't discussed with Blue where to meet. Her fingers were just reaching for her pocket, ready to extract her cell, when she felt a prickle on the back of her neck.

She spun around, and there he was.

All gorgeous and sexy as he leaned against a post near the entrance to the pier, way more attractive than he had any right to be in his blue jeans and navy tee. That man had a pair of thighs on him that made Anna's mouth water, especially since the memory of him naked, those thighs flexing beneath her as he stroked into her was permanently imprinted on her brain.

She pulled at the collar of her shirt, needing a little air.

Blue came close. "It's warm today in the city."

"Uh-huh."

Let him think that she was unused to the mid-seventy-degree

weather. Better that than him realizing she was playing a repeat of their night like it was some mental porn flick.

Cute.

Bring me some fudge and a side of X-rated fucking, please.

"You okay?" He touched her arm.

Anna forced a smile. "I'm great. My brain is just a little mush from this test I'm studying for."

"What class is it for?"

And just that easily, he relaxed her. Transforming her from a ball of nerves into a normal female who could hold a reasonable conversation. Plus, he'd also—at the same time as managing to get her to talk, listening to her story, laughing and commenting in the appropriate spots—somehow managed to lace her fingers with his and lead her to the boardwalk behind the line of popular shops.

By the time she'd whined her fill about tests and homework and the horrors of group projects, they were in a perfect position for sea lion viewing.

"Oh," she sighed. "They're adorable, aren't they?"

"Beyond adorable." He waggled his brows. "One might even say cute-tastic."

"Who?" She made a face. "*Who* would say that?"

"A two-hundred-and-two-pound professional hockey player?"

She gaped. "You don't weigh that much, do you?"

Blue gave her an affronted look and rubbed his hands across his stomach. "Don't you dare judge me just because I have a Twinkie problem."

"If Twinkies are known as the lean protein, whole grains, and greens diet Nutritionist Rebecca has you guys on." She raised one brow. "Don't forget that I've seen you naked. You don't have an extra inch of fat anywhere on you."

Indigo eyes heated. "Anywhere?"

Her cheeks were pink; she could feel it. "That's not fat, and you know it."

His smirk had her own lips tipping up in return. God, it felt good to laugh with someone.

"Is this the patented Anderson charm?"

More brow waggling. "It's the patented Anderson *something*."

She smacked him. "Well, take me and that patented Anderson *something* over to the fudge shop. I need chocolate and cookie dough."

He grinned, lips moving, but his words were drowned out by a sudden cacophony of barking and splashing on the platforms below. Still, as they wove their way through tourists and shops alike, Anna thought that his words might have been something along the lines of, "Is that the way to your heart?"

If she'd had the chance to respond, she would have said, "Yes. But you'll have to throw in some peanut butter, too."

And somehow the fact that she even considered an answer, joking or not—because she *did* really love peanut butter—didn't terrify her.

It *should* have terrified her.

But Anna found that with Blue's fingers laced through hers, warm and firm and secure, she wasn't scared.

In fact, for the first time in forever, she was hopeful.

FOURTEEN

BLUE

He was as giddy as a teenager on his first date.

And he kind of was.

On his first date, that was.

Because strolling hand in hand through a tourist trap, sharing an ice cream cone after having downed a volume of fudge that would make Nutritionist Rebecca red with rage, had never been Blue's idea of a good time.

But with Anna? It was everything.

She made him laugh, teasing him, busting his balls a bit, even got misty-eyed when a little girl ran right in front of them, yelling, "Daddy!" and was swept into her father's arms for a big hug. *So much range*, he thought. Which wasn't the right description, but he just didn't know how he could have ever thought that she'd been cold and distant.

She felt so much, if you only knew how to see it.

He squeezed her hand, smiling down at her as he wiped away a tear from the corner of her eye. "You're just a big softie, aren't you?"

A sniff, but she leaned closer, her shoulder snuggling beneath his arm so their sides pressed together, rising on tiptoe so she could whisper in his ear. "Tell anyone and I'll stab you with your own skate."

He burst out laughing. "Come on, Killer. Let's get some food that's not just refined sugar before Nutritionist Rebecca puts me on an all-kale diet."

"Speaking of the team," she said. "Max mentioned that the roster is looking really good this season."

"It is." Under the guise of bypassing a large crowd of camera-toting tourists, Blue tugged Anna a little closer. "We have a nice mix of new talent and experience. Plus, I've never seen Brit play better. She's really grown into a great goalie."

"When's your first game?"

He shrugged. "A couple of weeks. Preseason this weekend and a few more dotted in between."

"You guys don't play in those, right?" She tugged him across a street. "The restaurant is over here."

Blue followed. "The team will play, of course, but it is mostly rookies and training camp guys who'll fill the roster. Most of the main guys will take the rest before a long season." A shrug. "I'll try to hit one or two before the season officially starts, and depending on what Coach wants to do. It helps me find my legs."

"Makes sense. You guys have been practicing, but that's not the same as a game."

"Exactly." He pointed up at the sign, paint chipping, metal brackets almost rusted off. "So *this* is your place? The windows alone look like they'll give me tetanus."

She tsked. "There's that chicken rearing its ugly head again."

"You say chicken, *I* say smart enough to avoid food poisoning."

"Toe-may-toe, toe-mah-toe."

"Hilarious," he said, releasing her so he could pull open the door. "Come on, then. My poisoning awaits."

Anna surprised him by brushing a kiss across his cheek as she moved past him. "But it will be delicious poison."

Famous last words.

———

He got his wish to play in a preseason game the following week against the Flames.

It was a friendly match, with only a few glimpses of the intensity found in a regular game, but Blue relished the opportunity to get back on the ice, especially in front of a hometown crowd.

There was nothing like Gold fans, and the Gold Mine had become known as one of the loudest arenas in the NHL.

Even in the preseason, that was true, and Blue came off the ice that night on an adrenaline high that would have normally sent him straight to the bar to fuck off the extra energy.

Tonight, he could barely contain himself through the postgame talk, his Mandy-mandated—their trainer and sports medicine extraordinaire—cool-down routine, and the prescribed large glass of chocolate milk from Nutritionist Rebecca. The milk, especially with chocolate, had seemed crazy to him at first, but apparently it was scientific fact that the "magically delicious" substance was the best thing to drink after extreme physical exertion . . . or in his case, after a professional hockey game.

"Muscle fuel," Nutritionist Rebecca had called it.

Blue was just happy that he didn't have to drink those gross green shakes any longer.

Especially when it came to chugging it so he could get out of there—milk was infinitely more palatable than chunky, putrid green smoothies. He took one last gulp to finish off the glass then set it in the sink and took off for the showers.

"Blue?"

He turned to see Mandy, her baby asleep on one shoulder, and quickly closed the distance between them to carefully hug her. "I thought you were supposed to be on maternity leave for a little while longer."

A shrug. "The season's starting. I need to make sure the crew is in check."

"As if that was ever a concern," he teased.

She smiled, swaying slightly from side to side when little Madeline began to fuss. "It's true. They're doing great."

"But you couldn't stay away."

"That much is true. I love my job." Her eyes warmed. "And you guys are okay, too, I guess."

He patted Madeline gently on the back. "I'm going to shower and get out of here," he murmured. "I'll see you soon?"

"Yup."

He turned for the locker room.

"Oh, Blue?"

"Hmm?" he asked, striving for patience now when all he wanted to do was text Anna and see if she'd finished enough homework and would be free for dinner.

They'd eaten that evening a week before, laughing through soup-filled bread—she'd been right about it being beyond delicious—before he'd walked her to an Über and hugged her goodbye.

He'd wanted to *kiss* her goodbye but hadn't earned that right, and so he'd needed to be content with texting her daily and the possibility of meeting up soon for another meal.

Tonight.

Hence the hurrying through his responsibilities so he could get to his cell.

"You might not want to dash out of the arena as fast as you ran from the PT suite," Mandy said.

A frown drew his brows together. "Why?"

Had he forgotten about some team event?

"You may want to head up to the Family Suite after your shower." Her mouth twitched with amusement even as his heart pulsed with pain. But because Anna was probably the only person in the world who understood why the notion of the Family Suite wasn't exactly a positive for him, he was careful to keep the terseness out of his tone.

"Why's that?"

"There's a gorgeous blonde waiting for you up there."

His brows drew down in concern. He hadn't authorized anyone—

"A gorgeous blonde who bid a lot of your own money to save you from a predatory date auction."

It hadn't taken long for the news of his deception to get around the locker room.

Only fractionally faster than it had taken for the teasing to follow.

Blue's pulse jumped, his smile slipping out despite his efforts to the opposite. "I'll have you know it was beyond predatory."

"Carnivorous?" Mandy tilted her head to the side. "Man-eating?"

"Hush you." But he closed the distance between them and kissed her cheek. "Thanks."

"Treat her kindly, Blue," she murmured. "She's one of the nice ones."

He let the truth of his feelings show in his eyes. "I know."

She nodded. "Good." A beat. "So don't fuck it up."

"Language," he said with a chuckle.

"If Maddy's first word is fuck, it'll be Blane's fault."

"Sure, it will." And with one more pat to baby Madeline's back, Blue hauled ass to the showers.

Anna was here.

This time he would not fuck up.

FIFTEEN

ANNA

W hy had she come?

Brayden.

Or at least that was the convenient excuse she'd crafted.

Except Brayden had gone with Max and Angie, and she'd stayed and Blue hadn't texted her back, and now the wives and girl-friends were all staring at her with curious expressions on their faces and—

The door opened.

Her breath left her in a whoosh as Blue strode into the room. He was sexier than ever—because hello, suit and tie and well-fitting slacks—but add in shower-damp hair and some scruff, and her pussy was about to take out a billboard proclaiming its availability.

It remembered how good it had been.

Hell, *she* hadn't been able to forget that night with Blue.

Hence her *problem* with the man in question.

If problem could be defined as the man being sweet and kind and charming. He'd texted every day, even sent a delivery of food to her apartment when she'd had to turn him down for dinner because of an exam.

And now he was here, walking toward her with a warm smile that did all sorts of things to her stomach.

Kiss me, she thought and was disappointed when he didn't.

Anna knew it was probably for the best, that he was trying to be respectful, to prove to her that he'd meant what he'd said when he'd apologized. But her hormones wanted nothing to do with respect or apologies . . . unless either of those came with an eight-inch cock that was deep inside her, determined to bring her a copious amount of orgasms.

Fingers brushing the side of her throat, a stubble-rough mouth touching the skin below her jaw, a whisper that had her shivering. "What are *you* thinking?"

"How much I want you to fuck me again," she whispered back.

Blue reared back, eyes darkened with pleasure, even as humor crossed his expression. "You can't say stuff like that."

Her body drifted toward his. "Why not?"

The movement wasn't a conscious thought so much as they were like two magnets with opposite dipoles that were attracted to one another. Get them close enough and they'd slam together.

Either that or she'd fallen asleep with her math book over her face again and this was all a cruel dream.

"Killing me," he murmured, tongue flicking out to graze the shell of her ear.

"*Blue.*"

Breathless, but she ignored the fact that she sounded like a ninny. Such was the power of Blue, and she'd do best by accepting that rather than fighting it, especially when that acceptance brought orgasms.

"Pizza!" he declared, lacing their fingers together and tugging her toward the door. "Let's go get pizza."

"I don't think she wants *pizza*," one of the wives, Anna

thought it might have been Monique because the cackle that followed sounded like the former model. "She wants a good fu—"

The flash of movement caught her gaze, and she saw that Sara, Mike Stewart's wife and a former champion figure skater, had risen on tiptoe to clamp a hand over the much-taller Monique's mouth. "Go," she mouthed. "I can't hold her much longer."

Anna snorted and mouthed back, "Thank you," all while letting Blue lead her from the room.

"So pizza?" he repeated. "I know a really good place around the corner. They make their crusts from scratch. Never frozen and no canned—"

She reached up a hand, pressing one finger to Blue's lips. "I'm going to ignore the pizza commercial"—she gasped when he nipped at the digit. "Trouble," she murmured, "I was trying to ask if you can give me a ride home."

"Done."

"Great. Thanks."

"Any time." He held the elevator door for her then led her through the underground maze beneath the arena that led to the players' parking lot.

She smiled up at him. "And you can pick up one of those not frozen, not canned pizzas on the way, so long as I don't have to be the one to break it to Nutritionist Rebecca."

"What she doesn't know won't hurt her."

A redhead with a sour expression popped her head out of an open door.

"I heard that."

Blue winced but didn't stop walking, and Anna hurried to keep up.

"Whole wheat crust. No meat. No cheese," she called.

"Fine on the first two," he called back. "But I'm not giving up my cheese until the season starts."

Nutritionist Rebecca's sigh trailed them down the hall.

"Run," he muttered. "Before she takes it *all* away."

Anna giggled but didn't argue when he urged her to move faster.

She really wanted that pizza.

And the memory of laughing and running through the halls, clinging to Blue's hand as they moved was imprinted on her heart.

———

"I just can't do it!"

Brayden flopped onto his back dramatically, upsetting Anna's careful piles of notes and textbooks.

She sighed, moving them to the coffee table and restacking them. "Can't do what?"

"This!" He shoved a handout under her nose.

It was Thursday night, and they both had the following day off from school, but that didn't mean the homework stopped. She had a boatload of pages to read, notes to make, and Brayden to take care of.

Why had she thought jumping straight in with six classes would be a great idea?

Oh, yeah. Because she was crazy.

And then there was Brayden. Awesome, wonderful Brayden . . . who was driving her absolutely bonkers.

Bonkers with a capital B.

He didn't like that third grade had come with homework every night. He didn't like his new teacher any longer because she made him redo work in class if it was unreadable—which Anna thought was completely reasonable, considering how crappy Brayden's handwriting was.

But the thing he didn't like the most was that he and his best friend had been split up.

Probably because they'd spent the majority of the previous year acting like loons in class, and their teacher didn't wish their silliness on any of her workmates.

As someone who would hopefully soon become a teacher, she applauded that notion.

So anyway, third grade hadn't gotten off to the easiest start, especially considering all the changes at home.

Angie moving in. Anna not around as much.

While Bray was ecstatic to have Angie in his life, Anna knew those kinds of big life changes didn't come without growing pains.

And it didn't help that Max and Angie had slipped away for one more weekend before the season started, a quick jaunt down to San Diego that Anna suspected had a lot more to do with adding to their newly formed family and less to do with getting some time away from the city.

They'd offered to cancel their trip when they'd gauged Brayden's recent mood, but Anna had encouraged them to go.

This was their last chance for a break before the season really geared up.

And it would give her and Brayden some much-needed quality time.

The paper wiggled under her nose, threatening a paper cut, so she snagged the offending handout and glanced down at it.

After a moment, she looked up and somberly met Brayden's eyes.

God, he looked so much like Max.

It was uncanny . . . and also a distraction from her trying to improve Bray's mood. "This is serious," she said.

He nodded.

She pointed at her textbook, the one that could easily be used to knock out a three-hundred-pound linebacker. "So is that," she said, "and the fact that I need to get through about half of it before Monday."

His mouth dropped open. "What?"

"I know." She bumped her shoulder with his. "So, I think there is really only one thing to do."

"What's that?"

"Reset our brain with ice cream and *Angry Birds* then try our hand at homework in a couple of hours."

"Can we watch *Star Wars* instead?"

She groaned, having watched it close to three thousand—okay, she exaggerated, maybe only three *hundred*—times. "Again? I thought you really liked Bomb Bird."

Eyes widened into a pleading expression that got her every time. "Please?"

She pretended to sigh. "Can we at least get cookie dough ice cream if we do?" she asked, knowing it was his favorite. Not gonna lie, it was also *her* favorite, but sometimes cheering up her favorite eight-year-old had perks.

Smiles. Hugs. Calorie-laden ice cream.

"Yes!" He fist-pumped.

"Grab your jacket. I'll get my purse."

He was off and running for his stuff in an instant, and Anna took a few moments to stack her work to the side to do later. Probably during the movie, because he'd pick *Empire Strikes Back*—it was his, Angie's, and Max's favorite—and then Anna would strengthen her ability to quote its every line in her sleep.

She'd just zipped up her hoodie when her phone buzzed.

Dinner tonight?

Her breath caught.

Oh, Blue. She'd been determined to not like him from the start and then determined to not let him weasel his way in through her defenses . . .

Hopeless.

As in, that endeavor had been hopeless from the start.

Sorry, I can't. I'm watching Brayden this weekend.

They hadn't seen each other since their post-game pizza date, which had begun with a plethora of delicious cheese and carbs and ended with a chaste and friendly hug. But they had been texting or talking almost daily, and that was a feat in of itself.

She hated talking to anyone on the phone.

Except, Blue.

He made her laugh. *He* calmed her when she felt overwhelmed and stupid for thinking that this going back to school thing had been a crazy idea.

He'd become her friend.

And she couldn't remember the last time she'd let someone in enough for them to become that.

Max was one, of course, but easier for her to categorize since he'd also been her boss. Angie had been lovely, inviting her to dinners with her friends, including her, though there was a definite generation gap between them . . . or maybe a nerddom gap? Because Anna hadn't devoted a lot of time to *Star Wars* or *Harry Potter* or *Marvel* movies, and though the women in Angie's group had never made her feel unwelcome, Anna just hadn't connected fully.

Don't get her wrong.

Heidi, Kate, and Cora were fun and beautiful—on the inside as much as the outside—but sometimes people just didn't vibe.

Then there was Stefan, who was safely in the boss category and Brit, who was always nice but extremely busy with hockey and a variety of charities and endorsement deals. Brayden and Diane were different, she supposed, because they'd both gained lifelines straight to Anna's heart.

But neither of them really needed her any longer.

Diane had recovered and was dating her ex-husband, Pierre. Things were looking very serious between the two of them.

Brayden had Max and Angie, and Anna had to face facts. He was getting older, building his own life, his own friendships and activities that didn't revolve around her. He wasn't a little kid any longer.

Okay, yes, he was.

It was just that she had the feeling that his days of thinking she was super cool and fun to hang out with were limited.

Oh, that's right. I forgot Max was in San Diego. Have fun.

She smiled.

Ice cream is in my future, so fun is guaranteed.

"Why are you staring at your phone?"

"Oh." Anna jumped, quickly pocketing her cell. "No reason. I was just texting Blue back."

Brayden perked up. "Is he coming over?"

"No," she said. "I—um. No. He just asked if I would have dinner—" Too much information, but Anna was surprised enough by the enthusiasm in his voice that she was off her game.

"We should have pizza. You promised we'd have pizza one night, and Blue loves pizza." He began spinning in circles. "*And* Blue's favorite *Star Wars* movie is *Empire*, too!"

"Um. I thought *we* were going to—"

"You call him, and I'll finish my math homework so I'm ready when he gets here."

"—hang out this weekend."

Guess not.

Because Bray grabbed the previously offensive handout and settled down at the coffee table, pencil in hand. He glanced up after a minute. "Did you call him yet?"

Spinning at the turn in events, but also knowing that was just part of Life Lessons According to Brayden, she took out her cell and smiled at the response that had come in while she'd been stunned stupid by her charge.

It had better be cookie dough. :)

Her heart pulsed.

Because he remembered.

She was smiling when she tapped his name and hit the button to dial his cell.

"Anna?" he answered, partway through the first ring. "Everything okay?"

Which was the moment she realized *he* had been the one to text first every time, the only one to call, and that fact just scrambled her brain further, made her tongue twist.

"I— Um . . ."

"Sweetheart," Blue said. "Is everything okay with Brayden?"

"Oh, yeah," she said. "I'm sorry, he's fine. He . . . um just wanted me to ask if you wanted to come over for pizza and to watch *Star Wars* because he's conned me into watching *Empire* for the millionth time and, uh, I was just calling for that, but you're probably busy and . . ."

She trailed off, verbal vomiting finally coming to an end.

But seriously, thank God for small miracles.

Like her finally shutting her trap.

In fact, she should probably just hang up and pretend this whole call hadn't happened.

"I think maybe one of those brain-eating amoebas has crawled into my brain," she blurted.

Oh. My. God.

Silence was her only response.

"Or I'm having a stroke." Another blurt.

More silence.

Maybe *Blue* had hung up. Which was a perfectly reasonable response based on the crazy she was spouting.

Her finger hovered over the red button to end the call.

"I don't have to come over if you don't want me there," he said quietly.

That was what he'd deduced from her verbal barrage? That she didn't want him there?

Well, you were talking about strokes and flesh-eating amoebas, her brain pointed out.

Decidedly not helpful, brain.

His tone was gentle enough to snap her out of her own thoughts. "You can just tell Bray I'll have to catch up with him another time, okay?"

"No. *Stop.* I'm happy for you to come over if you want." She sighed and moved into the kitchen, pacing the narrow galley-shaped space. "I just—I'm not used to being the one to . . . *never mind,* this is stupid. I'm ordering pizza and ice cream from Door-Dash. If you want some cheese and carbs with me for the second time in a week, you know where I live. If not, Brayden and I are going to eat it ourselves."

A beat of quiet.

"Great," she said into it. "Okay, bye."

"Anna."

She hesitated, finger over the end button for a second time.

"I want to see you. I like spending time with you."

Simple words that meant . . . too freaking much.

"I also know that us spending time together after everything that happened still isn't the most comfortable for you," he said. "So my hesitation only comes from not wanting to push you into hanging out if you'd rather not see me."

These words were sweet and kind and altogether too much like martyrdom for her temper.

He was still chastising himself because he'd screwed up.

But they'd been over this. They'd talked. They'd hung. They'd moved past that night and the hurtful sentiments. She understood where he was coming from, trusted that he wouldn't say something like that again.

He'd spent the last few weeks proving that to her.

"If I didn't want to spend time with you, I'd say so," she said—okay, *snapped.*

So, *dammit,* the man could just accept an invitation gracefully.

"Come over if you want. Or don't. It's fine." She started to pull her cell from her ear when she heard him say her name again. "What?" she gritted out.

"I was just going to ask you for your apartment number."

Oh, right.

Because he knew her building but not her actual apartment number.

"2C. Call me when you get here, and I'll buzz you in."

"Will do, sweetheart."

He hung up, but not before Anna heard the smile in his voice.

God, she was so bad at this.

Sixteen

Blue

"So are you and Anna friends?" Brayden asked around a bite of pepperoni pizza.

Which was another thing he had to give Anna credit for.

Good taste in pizza.

Nothing crazy, like pineapple, just a simple but deliciously meaty topping. Or well, she'd kept her pineapple contained to her own personal pizza and had left him and Brayden with an unpretentious pepperoni meat-fest.

He smothered his smirk, knowing that if he'd said anything along the lines of meaty toppings or pepperoni meat-fest aloud in the locker room, the guys would have razzed him to no end. He would also probably have spent the subsequent weeks finding all sorts of "meaty" things hidden in various pieces of his equipment.

Hence the reason he always passed his words through his Dirty-Hockey-Player-Mind-Filter before saying anything aloud in the locker room.

It was just safer that way.

"Yeah," he said, when Brayden glanced away from the movie playing on the screen and up at him. "Anna and I are friends."

He'd arrived an hour before, just as the pizza guy had been leaving, an extra carton of cookie dough ice cream in hand because showing up empty-handed was rude.

Hell, who was he kidding?

He'd brought it to bribe his way into Anna's heart.

Or maybe just to see her smile.

That too.

Because when Anna smiled?

Damn, did he feel butterflies.

In this case, she *had* smiled, but it had been a harried and nervous flash of white before taking the carton and sweeping off into the kitchen, leaving him on the threshold.

That was fine.

Blue was patient, and he'd spent the last few weeks being especially so, but every text and conversation and second alone with Anna had brought him more clarity.

Anna was right.

For him, she was perfectly, absolutely right.

He would have lost his mind being with a woman who had no spark. He craved real affection. He needed fire and heat and teasing and . . .

He needed Anna.

Brilliant and funny Anna, her sweetness tempered by tart and heavy-duty concrete walls topped with barbed wire protecting what was underneath. Because those spiked strands were guarding something incredibly precious.

A huge heart.

So Blue was commencing Operation Win Anna Over, and he wouldn't give in until he managed to make it underneath those defenses.

He wouldn't settle until he'd staked a claim on her heart, until she accepted his in return.

He would win her over if it was the last thing he did.

"It's good to have friends," Brayden said with a nod, his gaze focused back on the screen and the fantastical battle on Hoth that had almost immediately put Anna to sleep.

The movie didn't capture his attention nearly as easily.

Not when Anna was curled up on the couch next to him, head pillowed on crossed arms, ponytail askew, pale pink lips slightly parted. She'd flitted around the apartment, grabbing plates and bowls, a bag of precut apples from the fridge, fussing with the stacks of books and the couch cushions before trying to wait on him and Brayden. If he'd been eight years old, he probably wouldn't have even noticed that all that darting around was from nerves, especially since Bray was more focused on getting the movie to stream. But Blue wasn't eight, and so he'd finally snagged everything from her hands, sat her down onto the fluffed cushions, and dished up two slices of pizza and some apples onto a plate.

Then he'd gotten Brayden settled before grabbing himself a few pieces.

He'd barely finished before Anna had jumped up again, declaring, "I'll get the ice cream."

Blue had followed her into the kitchen, watching as she scooped up three bowls of ice cream—into fresh bowls from the cupboard, rather than the ones she'd brought to the coffee table, but instead of commenting on that he'd made a mental note of the cabinet to return the dishes to later.

Jumpy.

She was so damned jumpy around him.

But he'd tried to remind himself that was a good thing.

Jumpy meant she was nervous. Nervous meant she felt something for him. He only needed to really worry if he got nothing from her—no nerves, no emotions at all.

So long as what she felt for him wasn't serial killer or stalker or crazy ex-girlfriend vibes, he could deal.

And continue to be patient.

However, all that jumpiness was also exhausting.

Case in point, the gorgeous blond female passed out on the couch next to him.

Brayden jumped up, fist in the air, yelling, "Yes!" as Luke took down an AT-AT. The sudden noise made Anna startle, almost toppling off the end of the couch.

Blue reacted in a second, launching forward to catch her, before tugging her back onto the cushions and scooting closer so she was cradled against his side. Her breath was unsteady as she peeled back her lids and peered up at him through pale lashes.

"You okay?" he asked.

She placed a hand over her heart. "I am now." She glanced at the table. "Death by textbook would have been really sad."

He smiled, started to release her and scooch back to his side of the cushions.

But then she did something that surprised him.

She nuzzled her cheek against his bicep and snuggled closer.

His own breathing went unsteady. "Anna?"

"Shh," she murmured. "I'm trying to remind myself why this is a terrible idea."

"Don't do that," he whispered, running a hand through her hair, stroking it across her back in gentle circles. "Remind yourself why it's a damned good one."

She froze, chin tilting up, eyes warming, lips parting.

He bent, mouth a hairsbreadth from hers.

Her hand came up, fingers weaving into the hair on his nape. Her tongue darted out, and *fuck it—*

"That's right, you jerks!" Brayden shouted. "You can't catch Han!"

They jumped apart, and Blue had no doubt her chagrined expression matched his. "Kid," he mouthed.

Cheeks flushing, she rolled her eyes.

But instead of moving away from him, instead of reinserting

the careful distance that had been between them the entire evening, Anna surprised him by resting her head on his shoulder.

His arms wrapped around her like it was the most natural thing in the world.

Or maybe it was.

Because this was Anna.

———

The ice was shit.

There was a heat wave in Northern California, and the arena was packed with seventeen thousand plus fans. Which meant the already warm air inside had gotten uncomfortably hot and the ice was soft . . . and that had been before there was an issue with one of the condensers, caused by a short-circuit due to a rolling brownout.

The generators had apparently kicked in, so the Gold Mine had power, but it was going to be a miserable game.

He, along with most of the other guys, had stripped off any and all extra layers after the pregame warm-up, but in all honestly, that wasn't going to make much of a difference, aside from making them pretend like they had done something to make the situation better.

Brit plunked down onto her knees on the floor in front of her station. Her bottom half was clad in her goalie pads and her top half a sports bra that was topped with several wet towels.

"Fuck, it's hot," she muttered.

"Feel you," Blue said. "I feel like I'm back in Florida where the rink never got cool."

She glanced over at him. "I didn't realize you were from Florida. I thought you played in Michigan."

Blue knelt next to her, stretching out his right quad. It had been particularly tight as of late, but Mandy had prescribed him a pregame movement routine that was helping. "I spent a summer in Florida." He touched his chest. "Military brat."

Brit's brows pulled together. "Why didn't I know that?"

He shrugged. "Not exactly something I broadcast."

"Blue—"

The concern in her voice was exactly what he didn't want before the first game of the season, and it was why he didn't share this kind of stuff, especially in the fucking locker room.

Now Brit was worried about him, and if she didn't play well, it would be his fault.

"Don't worry about it," he said. "It's"—he shook his head—"what it is."

She socked him. Hard.

His eyes darted to hers in surprise. "What the hell was that?"

"*It is what it is?*" she exclaimed. "What's going on in that pretty head of yours?"

"Leave it, Brit," he warned. "I don't want to mess you up before the game."

She flicked her ponytail over her shoulder, lifted one brow. "Really?"

A shrug. "Goalies are superstitious."

"Hockey players are superstitious. What you're trying to get at is the fact that goalies are weird."

"I didn't say that." But he was having a hard time biting back his smile.

"You didn't have to," she muttered. "But I'm not one of the weird ones. *I* can interact with other human beings before games in a semi-normal fashion."

Semi-normal?

He lost his battle with his smile.

"You just stand in the way of pucks on purpose."

A shrug. "Yeah, but so do you guys, *and* you do it without pads. So the crazy ones are . . ."

He lifted his palms in surrender. "I stand corrected."

Richie walked into the room, stacks of gloves just removed from the dryer in his arms. "Ten minutes to game time, folks."

"I'm not one of those goalies who doesn't want anyone talking to her before the game," she said, pulling off the towels and shrugging into her chest protector.

"You don't need to visualize?" he teased.

"Visualize my stick up your—"

"Hi, love," Stefan said, plunking down in the spot on Brit's other side. "Threatening the guys again?"

"It's the only way to get us to play good," Max called from the other side of the room. "Pure terror."

Brit rolled her eyes. "Y'all are hilarious."

Max bowed. "And I thank you for your commendation."

"I'm surrounded by idiots," Brit declared.

"Hey—" Max began.

"All right, all right," Bernard said, cutting him off as he strode into the room. He wore a black suit and bright yellow tie and appeared more determined than ever. Blue knew the feeling, could almost sense in his bones that this season was different somehow.

Not necessarily that the stakes were higher or the roster was better, but that maybe this could be their year.

Internally, he rolled his eyes. This was the same feeling as *every* year.

Possibility.

That *this* was their season.

But eighty-two games was a lot of hockey, so who knew what the cards held.

"Let's focus, people," Bernard continued. "I know it's hot, but I want us to go out there tonight and play our game. Chase down loose pucks, finish checks, make the easy play, and don't force the puck . . ." He listed a few more items as they all finished suiting up. "Let's do this right, guys and gal."

Blue straightened and rolled out his shoulders, adrenaline beginning to pump through his body.

Fuck, yes.

It was time to play some hockey.

He stood up and followed Brit as she led them down the hall, snagging his stick from the rack as he went.

The roar of the crowd intensified with each step until it was almost deafening as they burst through the door leading onto the ice.

He did his couple of laps—Brit wasn't wrong in teasing him about hockey players being superstitious, then skated to the blue line for the national anthem. A few minutes and one semi-decent rendition later, he was at center ice, stick hovering just above the red dot and waiting for the ref to drop the puck.

The whistle sounded.

He and the other center jockeyed for stick position and then . . .

The puck dropped.

Blue flew into motion, winning the draw back to Max who carried it up a few strides before sending a pass over to Kevin, Blue's left wing. Kevin was *fast*. He skated the puck into the zone and dumped it deep.

Which was when Blue got to work, sprinting into the corner and getting a hard hit to his back for his trouble. But he came out with the puck and managed to get it over to Kevin, who took a shot on net that—unfortunately—the goalie stopped easily.

And just that quickly, Blue's shift was over.

Heart pounding and sweat already dripping down his spine, he and the rest of his line skated to the bench.

It was a constant push-pull of hustling up the ice then rushing back, of dodging hits and giving them, of skating hard and skating *really* hard. Add in the heat, and he was seriously sucking wind by the time the third period rolled around.

Blue happened to look up at the Jumbotron. On its screen was one of those scales that climbed higher the louder the crowd cheered. But that wasn't what caught his attention. Because interspersed with that climbing gauge were shots of fans cheering—

Anna.

Whoever was running the camera chose that exact moment to cut to *Anna*.

She was in the stands, wearing a Gold jersey and sitting next to Brayden and Angie. She wasn't wearing a stitch of makeup and didn't have anything particularly revealing on, but seeing her having so much fun just jumping up and down next to Bray and cheering like a madwoman, and she was the most beautiful thing he'd ever laid eyes on.

"Dude." Trevor, a winger from the second line, punched him. "*Dude.*"

Blue tore his eyes from the screen and glared at Trevor. "What?"

"Dude, get your ass off the bench."

He glanced from Trevor to the ice, saw that Kevin and Stevie were both staring at him.

"Fuck," he muttered, hopping on and deliberately not looking toward the other end of the bench where Bernard and the other coaches were no doubt wondering what in the fuck he was doing.

There was no way to play it off now, nothing to be done for it. He just had to get to the face-off dot and play some fucking hockey.

The opposing center smirked at him. "Nice of you to join us."

"Fuck off," he said, partly—okay, not really at all—under his breath.

But there wasn't time for a response.

The puck hit the ice and Blue won it back to his defenseman. A quick pass to the side and Kevin snagged it, skating it into the zone. Sticks collided with sharp cracks, players yelled to their teammates, fans screamed, and Blue . . . slipped in behind the defense.

Kevin saw him, they had a flash of eye contact, a heartbeat of perfect communication, before Kevin made a killer pass and got the biscuit right onto Blue's stick.

Maybe the easiest goal he'd ever score.

With the barest flick of his wrists, the puck was in the back of the net.

His teammates rushed him, and they all crashed into the boards. He couldn't hear anything aside from his pulse pounding in his ears, but he happened to look up and see that the guys had pushed him into the glass directly in front of Anna and Brayden.

She winked down at him and mouthed, "Lucky shot."

And Blue laughed his ass off all the way to the bench.

SEVENTEEN

ANNA

She waved off Angie and Max's offer of a ride, ignoring the knowing look on Angie's face and the smirk on Max's.

She also ignored the, "Baby Blue said he'd wait for you at his car."

And Angie's giggle that followed.

Anna shook her head, because that was awfully presumptuous of Baby Blue to assume she would just come when called, but she didn't say anything to Max. Instead, she just gave Brayden another squeeze and then walked across the parking lot to Blue's car.

He was standing next to the passenger's side door of his sleek black sedan, and damn, but she loved this man in a suit.

"Hi," she murmured.

"How much trouble am I in?"

How did he know what she was thinking?

She managed to bite back her laugh and narrowed her eyes at him.

"Uh-oh," he said, brushing his thumb along her jaw. "That much?"

Turning her head so she could press a kiss to his palm, she murmured, "*So* much."

Fingers down her cheek, her throat, across both collarbones. "Should I remind you that I scored the game winner tonight?"

Laughter bubbled up in her chest. "Is that the patented Anderson charm at work?"

His mouth grazed hers. "Only if it's working."

Anna's heart was pounding, and desire pooled low in her belly. They'd been working toward this for weeks now. Talking and texting and hanging out with nary a non-platonic gesture in sight.

Building trust.

Making ties.

And somehow, that didn't scare her anymore.

The idea of forging a bond with Blue had become . . . safe?

Or if not that exactly, then it was some combination of comfort and shelter—

Who was she kidding? It was also heat, so much underlying heat brewing beneath the surface that Anna felt as though she'd be incinerated or perhaps scalded by the intensity of how much she wanted him.

It had been so fucking good between them.

And she wanted more.

Which is why she nipped at his bottom lip and said, "Why don't you kiss me and find out?"

No hesitation. No questions asking if she was sure. No mutual agreements that this would be a horrible idea. Not this time. Because *this* time was different. This time around she knew Blue better . . . and maybe she also knew *herself* better.

His lips slanted across hers and hers were already parted, her tongue darting into his mouth to dance with his. He slid an arm around her hips, yanking her flush against his chest and deepening the kiss—

A horn blared.

They jerked apart as Brit and Stefan drove by shouting, "Get a room!"

Blue muttered something . . . well, something *blue* under his breath, but slowly released her and opened the passenger door. "We should—"

She threw her arms around his neck and kissed him.

Teeth and tongue, heat and hard muscles, and it was fucking amazing. No one had ever kissed her the way Blue did. Like she was the sexiest thing he'd ever seen, like he couldn't get enough.

Like the thing he wanted most in the world was her.

Eventually, her lungs screamed for air and she pulled back. He rested his forehead to hers, breaths coming fast.

"Come on," he told her. "I'll drive you home."

He helped her into his car, buckling her seat belt for her even though she obviously could do it herself. It was funny, they'd only spent a few nights together, but the fact was she liked it when he did those small things for her. When he was holding the door or brushing his fingers over her shoulder when he left the room or even just buckling her seat belt, she knew he was showing her that he cared.

Which made her next decision as easy as choosing chocolate cake over Brussels sprouts.

They were fairly quiet as he made the drive to her apartment. All of the post-game traffic had dispersed by the time he'd finished with his cool down, the press, and his shower and so the drive was also quick.

But when he began to pull up to the curb, Anna touched his arm.

"You know the best thing about this apartment?"

He shook his head.

"It has two designated parking spots," she said.

He froze before glancing her way, smirk teasing the corners of his mouth. "So, what are you saying?"

She shrugged. "Just that I've got this virtual treasure trove of

San Francisco parking availability, and it's a shame that no one is using it."

A somber nod. "Such a shame."

"I don't know if you can think of anyone who might be interested in using it?"

Another nod, this one decidedly more mischievous. "I'll call Kevin. He's always complaining about having to find street parking."

"Blue!"

He caught her fingers with his, pressed a kiss to the back of them. "Where's the entrance?"

A minute later, he'd pulled into the normally empty spot next to her little sedan and turned off his car. Silence descended, and she wondered if her parking spot invitation needed to be extended to a going upstairs invitation.

But just as she'd opened her mouth to ask him to come up, he turned to face her.

"You sure?"

And her heart melted.

"We've been building toward this for a while, don't you think?"

"We can *keep* building toward it." He tucked a strand of hair that had escaped her ponytail behind one ear. "Because if I come up . . ."

She nodded. "Does it make a difference if I *want* you to come up?"

His eyes softened. "It makes *every* difference, but I also don't want to mess this up. I hurt you before—"

"What happened to the confident, bordering on cocky man who gave me a night of multiple orgasms?" she teased.

"He realized that he was kind of an asshole." Blue scowled then pushed open his door and shut it again before she could respond. Probably for the best because she would have agreed that he *had* been an asshole. But he was a reformed asshole now, and Anna was crazy about him.

"Come on, darlin'," he said, opening her door and extending a hand.

"I like this asshole," she whispered when he tugged her to her feet and straight into his arms. She *really* liked the way he made her feel, how he held her like she was something important.

He laughed and pressed a kiss to the top of her head. "I do love that sharp tongue."

The momentary image of her using her tongue to trace every part of Blue's body distracted her from his words. But only for a moment before she recounted what he'd said and then what she'd said before that.

Whoops.

Okay, so the closed door hadn't stopped her from blurting out an agreement, but at least Blue didn't seem to mind.

In fact, he appeared entertained, amusement dancing in the blue depths of his eyes.

She bit her lip.

He groaned. "Lead the way, trouble," he said and released her from his embrace, taking her hand instead.

"Hmph." But she smiled as she led him up the stairs to her apartment.

"Of the best kind," he murmured halfway up the first flight.

"Damn straight—" The words caught off when she turned around and saw him staring at her ass. "Eyes up here."

He pinched her cheek. And not the one on her face.

"Fuck, no. Not when I've got this gorgeous thing swaying in my face."

Anna huffed, continuing up the stairs. "And here I thought you were watching my back." A beat. "Or maybe my shoulders."

"Back*side* maybe, but—" His words cut off and she felt his stare. It was a heavy, tangible thing. "*Anna.*"

She didn't turn around, couldn't turn around. Not when she'd brought his attention to the fact that 'Anderson' was emblazoned on the back of the jersey she wore and yes, she knew it was silly, but now that he'd noticed it . . .

All the nerves.

"Baby," he murmured.

More steps. More climbing. They were almost to her floor.

"I—*eek!*"

She was suddenly in the air, legs and arms flailing as Blue scooped her up and cradled her against his chest.

"Arms around my neck, sweetheart."

Breathless, she did as ordered, her fingers weaving into the bristles on his nape. She loved the way those shorn hairs felt. "You should put me down. I'm heavy and don't want you to hurt yourself one game into the season."

He snorted and pressed a kiss to the top of her head, ignoring her and instead nuzzling the sensitive skin of her throat. "Like the jersey, baby."

Her pulse settled as he began to climb the remainder of the stairs. "You're giving me all the endearments today, aren't you?"

"I'm going to give you *something*," he murmured, making her giggle.

"My keys?" she asked innocently, trying to shift so she could reach into her purse, since they'd now reached her door.

"Hmm." He leaned against the wall, pinning her between the surface and the firm expanse of his chest. One hand traced upward along the outside of her leg, drifting over the back pockets of her jeans. "Are they in here?"

"I think you thoroughly examined *that* on the stairs."

"That was a visual inspection only," he said, calloused fingers slipping under the jersey's hem then down beneath the waistband of her jeans. He traced the top of her ass, the roughened fingertips making her shiver. "Hmm." He pretended to think. "Maybe I just need to search lower."

Her breath came out in a long, slow hiss.

"Search inside my apartment," she demanded.

"I don't know," he said, removing his fingers from her jeans, but not from beneath the jersey. He kept pressing forward, holding her against the wall with one arm and his lower body, and while that felt fabulous, it was his free hand that was so devastating to her concentration. "These walls look pretty thin. I remember how you like to scream, sweetheart. Maybe we should continue this another day at my place."

"My walls are plenty th-thick."

Rough fingers against bare skin.

Fluttering movements on the outsides of her breasts.

Her breath caught when a warm palm cupped her over her bra. "Blue," she moaned.

"Like my name on your lips, baby." Then his hand was gone.

"Wh-what?"

The reason for the absence of his delicious hand was evident a few seconds later, after he'd managed to extract her keys from her purse then unlock the door to her apartment. One minute she was on the outside of her place, the next she was inside, flush against the wood panel and Blue's mouth slamming down onto hers.

Fire.

One touch of his mouth, and her nerves erupted with heat.

Pleasure danced down her spine, coiling into a tight mass below her belly button. Her thighs were spread wide, his hips pressing against her, but it didn't stop them from suddenly throbbing with a deep-seated need to press together, to find some way to slake the aching emptiness inside of her.

"Fuck, baby," Blue groaned against her mouth, hips rocking, hard cock pressing the seam of her jeans against her clit.

She cried out and threw her head back, arching her back and trying desperately to get closer.

Too many layers.

Skin.

She needed skin.

Blue moved with the lightning-quick speed she'd witnessed on the ice, tearing her jersey over her head before dropping to his knees. Somehow, she managed to stay on her feet, but it was pure luck.

Or maybe, his hands were what kept her aloft. One palm flat against her belly, a scalding brand, as the other worked at the button on her jeans. Then her zipper.

Then tugged her jeans down to her ankles.

He lifted one foot and then the other, removing her shoes and socks before her jeans followed suit. She stood before him in her bra and panties, a set she'd put on earlier that evening because part of her knew it would come to this.

The draw between them wasn't one and done.

It was more. Deeper.

She needed *him* more. And deeper.

"God, I love you in lace," he muttered and nipped the inside of her right thigh. She jumped, but he had her, that large palm rubbing up and down, up and down. She arched, wanting him to pick a direction and stick with it, to delve his fingers between her thighs or to bring them up to her nipples and pinch and tease like he'd done that night several months ago.

Anything but this slow and steady up and down, up and down.

She lifted shaking fingers to the band of her bra and undid the clasp.

Blue's growl made her shiver, that ache between her thighs even stronger.

"Touch me," she moaned.

And thank God, he did. His mouth latched onto her nipple, his fingers slipped beneath her panties, caressing the damp heat of her. In less than thirty seconds she was crying out, hips jerking, pleasure spiraling outward from her center. Then he did something with his thumb and in thirty seconds more, she was summiting the precipice, screaming as she plummeted over the edge into orgasm.

"Fuck, you're beautiful," he said, tugging her panties down and pressing his mouth to her center.

He didn't give her a second to catch her breath, not one moment to recover from the orgasm, not a heartbeat to remember her name or what city she lived in. Instead, he slid his tongue up through her folds, circling the sensitive bud of her clit before sucking it firmly into his mouth.

Lightning flashed behind her eyes, and her knees gave out.

She probably wouldn't have felt a damned thing, even if she *had* crashed to the ground, the sheer volume of pleasure was so great. But Anna didn't get that far because the moment she began to slip, Blue caught her.

He broke her fall, guiding her to the entry rug, his mouth barely leaving her pussy before he was right back at it, shouldering in between her thighs, fingers spreading her wide and mouth taking her right back up to the edge.

"Oh God!" she cried.

And that was the last rational thought Anna had before she exploded again.

Pleasure spiraled up and out from her center, spreading to her limbs and making them heavy. Her brain blinked out, nothing but blissful blackness filling it for one long moment.

It wasn't until she found herself almost six feet in the air, in Blue's arms, that consciousness began to return.

He carried her down the hall and into her bedroom, setting her gently on the mattress. She propped herself up onto one elbow as he stripped out of his suit jacket and tossed it on the chair. His shirt came next, the crisp white cotton separating to reveal a chest she wanted to lick like a fucking Popsicle as he made quick work of the buttons.

That too landed on the chair.

By the time his fingers reached for the button on his slacks, Anna had regained feeling in her legs.

She pushed off the mattress and knelt in front of him, loving how his gaze went somehow even hotter as she did so. "Let me."

He hissed when she fumbled with the button, the hard length of him pulsing against her palms, the squares of his ab muscles standing out in sharp relief as he stood perfectly still while she worked at the clasp. She sensed that he was teetering on the edge of control, but couldn't bring herself to slow down or tread carefully. He was heated granite beneath the cotton, and she needed, absolutely *needed* his cock in her hands, her mouth.

Carefully, she lowered the zipper.

His cock sprang out, and Anna couldn't wait any longer. She stretched up to take it into her mouth.

They both groaned at the contact, Blue's hand coming to the back of her head, not pushing but gently holding her as she worked him deep into her throat. In and out, in and out. So long that she needed both hands and her mouth to hold the whole length of him, so thick that he made her jaw ache after only a few strokes.

She'd work on that, though.

Because Blue was losing patience.

One flick of her tongue on the underside of his head and her mouth was tugged free. Another squeeze of her hand had the offending limbs brushed away. Wiggling closer had her tossed back onto the mattress, Blue between her spread thighs.

He tore open a condom, rolled it on, and then flashed her what only could be described as a sinful smile.

"Time to test those walls, baby."

He pushed home.

She screamed.

And based on all the disgruntled pounding from her next-door neighbors, it turned out that Anna's walls weren't thick enough after all.

EIGHTEEN

BLUE

Sunlight streamed in through windows and a beautiful blonde was snuggled in his arms.

Also known as heaven.

Anna smelled like roses, her skin was like silk, and her . . . pussy was pressed directly against his thigh and getting wetter by the second.

Which wasn't helping his morning wood situation, especially when her hips tilted, and one bare thigh rubbed against his cock. Blue held his breath, forcing himself to stay still.

At least until one slender hand drifted down his chest to cup him.

Eyes flashing open, he caught a glimpse of her smirk.

"You're intent on tormenting me."

She placed a hand on his chest, pushed up slightly. Well, pushed up enough that he got an excellent view of her breasts bobbing as she shrugged. "Maybe." Another shrug that kept his gaze locked on those glorious nipples. "Maybe not."

He flipped their positions, took one into his mouth.

"Fuck!" she cried, hands weaving into his hair, thighs parting to let him slip between.

Moisture spread over his dick, hot wet heat that was so fucking tempting.

He released her nipple, scrabbled for the condom he'd left on her nightstand . . . but it wasn't there.

Shit.

He leaned back, glancing over the side of the bed, the movement bringing their hips into better alignment, and it was so damned tempting to shift slightly, to slide home.

Condom.

Fuck, he *needed* that condom.

But it wasn't on the nightstand.

Or the floor.

Or the pillow beside them.

"Blue," Anna moaned, writhing against him. "What's the matter?"

He was panting now. "Condom," he said. "I can't find it."

Her eyes were glazed, hips undulating, so hot and wet against him. "I'm on the pill," she said between rapid breaths. "Clean." A sucked in breath as he cupped her breast. "You?"

"I'm clean." He bit back a groan and tried to focus. "Tested before the season started."

"Good." Her thighs dropped open. "Then fuck the condom and just fuck me."

He froze, the words making a red haze form behind his eyes. He'd never had sex without a condom before, but this was Anna and—

God, he wanted her so much.

"Blue?" she asked, her voice almost hoarse.

"You sure, baby?"

A nod. "Only if you are—"

He pushed into that slick heat.

Holy. Fucking. Shit.

Never had anything felt as good as sliding into Anna's wet pussy with no barriers between them. She was scorching, the sopping evidence of her desire making every rational thought flash away into nothing.

"Oh fuck," she groaned, head thrashing from side to side, hips bucking up and—

Blue didn't think any longer.

He *couldn't* think.

He just moved.

Pulling out and sliding in, angling his hips so he hit the spot that never failed to make her gasp and doing it over and over again with absolutely no quarter. Because this? It was fucking incredible, and even though he'd made love to her twice the night before, Blue knew he'd be lucky to last another thirty seconds.

Thankfully, Anna didn't need more than that.

She wrapped her legs around his hips, met him stroke for stroke, and just when he was worried that he might fall over the edge before her, she exploded with a loud scream that had her neighbors pounding against the wall in protest.

Again.

Not the he could summon a fuck because one more stroke and he was over the edge.

"Next time," he said, when he had finally managed to catch his breath. "We go to my place."

Anna was face down on the mattress, limp and sated, but his words had her making a valiant effort to roll over. In the end, he helped her, tugging her up against his chest. She smiled and patted his cheek, eyes already sliding closed. "Your place," she agreed and fell headlong into sleep.

Blue wasn't far behind her.

———

The next couple of weeks were a blur, filled with hockey and travel and long, pleasurable nights with Anna whenever they could manage.

At his place.

Mostly.

So her neighbors didn't hate him *too* much.

He snorted, knowing that was totally false but not caring in the least. Not when he'd gotten to spend so much time with Anna, not when seeing her was so fucking incredible.

Every minute with her seemed to lace them closer, and he thought . . . well, he thought that he might love her.

Idiot, he imagined her teasing him.

But a lovestruck one.

So he smiled, tucking that buoyant feeling close to his heart and pulled out his cell to send her a text.

Dinner?

She hadn't been able to make it to the game because of a big exam the following day, but he'd hoped to at least squeeze in dinner, since the team was flying out early the next morning for an extended road trip.

Knowing the response wouldn't come immediately if she was knee-deep in studying, Blue went through his post-game routine and showered before checking his cell again.

No response.

Weird.

He knew she'd been expecting him to text since they'd talked about it that morning. Maybe she'd fallen asleep?

You okay?

Blue waited a half-hour, finishing up some outstanding things as he hung around the arena. Hell, who was he kidding? He was just killing time on the off chance she'd text back and so he wouldn't have to change directions and drive to her place, closer to the arena, but also in the opposite direction of his house.

Still nothing.

He sent one more message as he walked to his car, knowing she'd probably crashed and fallen asleep with her study guide stuck to her forehead, but not able to stop a sinking feeling from forming in his gut.

I know you're probably sleeping, but text me as soon as you get this, so I don't worry.

It seemed to take an eternity, but his phone finally buzzed with a message as he started up his car.

I'm so sorry. I fell asleep. I'm too tired for dinner tonight. Rain check?

Blue released a relieved breath. See? Worried for no reason.

Of course. I'll text you tomorrow.

A buzz.

Don't text me. I'll text you.

His brows pulled together into a frown.

I don't want my cell going off during class.

Um. But before he could process that, his cell buzzed one more time.

:)

Blue texted back, promising to wait to hear from her, then another, responding to her goodnight. They were all the right words, all the right sentiments, and yet he couldn't forget that smiley face.

Somehow it was all wrong.

Somehow *everything* suddenly felt wrong.

NINETEEN

ANNA

She was freaking the fuck out.

Yes, she'd had an exam that morning.

No, that wasn't what had frightened her.

She was late.

As in. She. Was. Late.

Groaning, she unlocked her car door and plunked into the driver's seat. It had been barely a month since the Gold season had gotten under way, and she and Blue had spent as much time together as possible . . . which meant they'd spent as much time fucking as possible.

Without condoms.

Which she'd never done before.

But it was Blue and . . . shit, she didn't *have* any other reasoning aside from the fact that it was Blue, and he made her feel safe and protected. Like he would always be there for her. No matter what.

And now she was late.

Her eyes stung and she plunked her head down onto her steering wheel. If she was—

Fuck, if she could barely think it, how was she going to say it?

If she *was* pregnant—there, mission complete. Gold star for her for managing to think the word, but that didn't matter at all, did it? Because the only thing that truly mattered was: what the hell was she going to do?

She'd just gone back to school.

Was barely one semester in and mere months away from starting the program at her first choice.

Babies were a hell of a lot of work, and she didn't have time to be pregnant, let alone to devote every waking moment to their needs. She'd spent the last few years doing just that—spending all of her energy focusing on first, Diane, and then second, Brayden. She was done.

She wanted to focus on herself for a change.

But—Anna released a shuddering sigh and pressed her hand to her stomach—she might be pregnant.

And that changed *everything*.

Not to mention the fact that all of the changes she'd been thinking about were on her end. She hadn't even begun to consider what Blue might think, how a baby at this point in the season—or more importantly, at this point in his life would transform everything.

She bit her lip, tears burning the back of her throat. He hadn't even wanted her at first, what if he didn't want—

Her phone buzzed.

"Shit," she said, wiping her eyes with the back of her hand and glancing down at her cell, hoping it wasn't Blue, praying that if it was, she would come up with a few magic words that could explain the situation and would put *every*thing to rights.

But it wasn't Blue.

Instead it was—

"Diane?" she asked, swiping her finger across the screen and hurriedly putting her cell up to her ear. "Is everything okay?"

Stefan's mom was as chipper as ever. "Fine, darling. I was just hoping that you might be close by. I made spaghetti and—"

Suspicion instead of pure unadulterated terror twisted in Anna's gut.

"What do you want?" she asked, not coldly, but directly. Because she knew Diane's tricks by now, and spaghetti . . . well, that meant something was up.

Diane huffed, but her response was tinged with amusement. "It's been too long since I've seen you."

And silence.

Into which Anna asked, "And?"

"*And* I heard you were seeing Blue."

Well, now that was to be determined, wasn't it?

She sighed. Her last class had finished and all her exams complete. She didn't have any excuse to stay away, and honestly? She *wanted* to talk to someone who wasn't the voices inside her brain.

"I'll be there in twenty."

Diane squealed. "I'll open the wine."

Anna's "Better not," came after the *click* of the other phone cutting off.

———

Diane had taken over Stefan's bungalow when he and Brit had moved into a larger house in a nearby gated community, but the cute cottage had definitely been more Diane's style than her son's from the get-go.

Another reason why Stefan was so great.

He might have been living over a thousand miles away, Diane having refused to move to California initially, but he'd still bought a place where she could be comfortable.

Cheery windows faced the street and the porch was large and adorned with brightly colored flower pots. A rocking chair sat in one corner, along with a small table that Anna could even see from the street was stacked high with paperbacks. Nothing was particularly neat or overtly organized, but everything had a spot, including the riotous chaos of the flowers filling the pots.

The whole space was Diane.

Perpetually happy and endearing.

She'd opened the front door before Anna had gotten out of her car and was barreling down on her, a five-feet nothing bundle of energy that swept her into a tight hug.

"It's been too long, dear." She snagged Anna's hand and dragged her into the house. "Come on then. You look like you need a good meal."

Probably because her stomach was unsettled.

Or one might say nauseous.

Her heart twisted in on itself, anxiety pulsing within her. Fuck, what was she going to do?

Diane took one look at Anna's face and moved a little faster, not stopping the forward propulsion until Anna was plunked safely into a kitchen chair.

No chipper conversation. No filling the air with gossip as was her habit.

Just silence.

Until she sat down across from Anna and said, "So you and Blue, huh?"

And cue tears.

"Oh no"—a screech as the chair pushed back, and a moment later, arms were wrapped tightly around her—"Sweetie, I'm sorry. I didn't mean to push."

"It's not—" She sniffed, reaching up to scrub at the corners of her eyes. "It's not you. I'm just upset and . . . *hormonal*."

Diane leaned back, raised a brow.

"I mean," she hurried to say. "I haven't taken a test or

anything, and I'm late, and—" There the tears went again. "I'm just going back to school, and Blue and I are so new . . ."

"You're worried he'll break up with you."

Anna paused and considered that, but only for a moment. "No," she said. "I don't think he would." This wasn't his plan, and he might need some time to process the sudden change in circumstances, same as her, but Blue liked kids, and when they'd discussed it, he had been very clear that he wanted a house full of them.

Someday.

That was the crux of the problem.

Because what if someday was here?

"So *what?*"

"It's too damned soon," she murmured. "We haven't been dating long enough—."

Diane shook her head. "Not it. Try again."

"I'm going back to school. I don't know how'll I'll manage—"

"Pretty excuse," Diane said, "but still not the real reason you're scared."

She sighed, knowing Diane was right, and since she was one of the few people Anna had confided in about her childhood, she let out the truth that was sitting like a heavy boulder on her chest. Because—

"I'm not fixed yet," she whispered. She was working on it, had made a lot of progress over the last few years, but she still had so much baggage, so much fear that the moment Blue learned about her childhood—how she'd been left then passed around time and time again because no one wanted her—he'd realize he didn't want her either.

"So what you're saying is that you have no worth."

"What?" Anna's eyes shot up from the table. "I—"

A fist on the table. "No," Diane said. "What you're telling me is that rather than your childhood being something terrible and tragic that has no bearing on you as a person, instead of it being something you should be so damned proud to have overcome, what you're saying is that because you were in foster care you have no worth?"

"I—" She shook her head. "*No.*"

"So why would Blue see it as any different?"

"I—" A sigh. "He has this plan, this image of someone perfect in his head. Someone sweet and kind and soft. I'm not that. I've got barbs and sharp points and—"

"Ah."

Anna frowned.

"I get it now." Diana put her hand on top of Anna's "You're waiting for him to leave you."

"No. *Yes.*" She blinked rapidly. "I'm not the person he imagined himself with. I can *never* be her."

"And yet he wants to be with *you.*"

Fingers squeezed Anna's before Diane pushed out of her chair. Noise of plates being pulled from a cupboard, from a pan lid being lifted, pasta being served up filled the space between them. By the time a plate was in front of Anna, her tears had dried.

"You're really special, dear. But you need to believe that here." Diane touched Anna's temple. "And here." A tap above her heart. "Until then, you're going to feel like shit."

That startled a laugh out of her. "Really? That's how you're going to end our inspirational talk?

She stuck a fork in Anna's hand. "Eat. And yes, because the person you should be having this conversation with is Blue."

And . . . gauntlet dropped.

Anna made a face. "I hate it when you're right."

Diane tugged the end of her ponytail before sitting down across from Anna, a full plate in front of her. She looked healthier than Anna had ever seen her. Skin rosy, cheeks full instead of sunken.

"You look good."

A wave of her hand. "I'm old. Wrinkled." A pretend sniff. "And you never call. You never visit."

Anna's lips twitched. "You're busy with Pierre."

"Pish," Diane muttered. "*Pierre*. That man is in the doghouse."

For some reason that made Anna smile. "What'd he do this time?"

"He bought me flowers."

She snorted. "Oh the humanity."

Diane rolled her eyes. "I'd told him not to, and he went ahead and sent that extravagant arrangement anyway." She pointed at a gorgeous vase of roses and daisies that took up a good portion of the opposite counter.

"Aren't daisies your favorite?"

A sniff, albeit a real one this time. "Yeah, so?" Diane elaborated when Anna just lifted a brow. "*So*, I told him not to send anything when he was gone." She shoved her plate away. "I told him I needed to think about it, and he ignores me anyway, trying to woo me with stupid daisies."

"They're gorgeous daisies," Anna said, rather helpfully, despite Diane's huff. "What's he trying to get you to agree to?"

"He wants to move in together"—she lifted one finger, affecting a rather good impression of Pierre—"and said, I quote, 'Neither of us are getting any younger.'" She glared when Anna laughed. "It's not funny. He might as well have said that we were going to die soon, so come in and be my live-in housekeeper."

Anna couldn't hold back her giggles, and this time Diane joined in. "If we're being real here, I think Pierre can afford a housekeeper."

The owner of the Gold—and Stefan's dad because, yes, things were complicated—was a billionaire many times over. He could afford an army of staff if he so desired.

"The man has the romantic capabilities of an ant," Diane grumbled.

"I don't know about that," Anna murmured. "But he does have good taste in flowers."

A sigh. "Yes," Diane agreed. "Yes, he does." Another sigh. "He offered to move in here."

"What?" Anna's mouth dropped open. "*Really?*"

Pierre had a penthouse in the city. One that took up an entire top floor of a huge high-rise.

"That's huge."

Diane nodded. "I know."

"So," she said, squeezing her friend's hand. "What are you waiting for?"

"Same thing as you, I suppose."

Anna's lips curved. "Never let me off the hook, do you?"

"That what friends do."

"No." She pushed out of her chair and hugged Diane tightly. "That's what moms do," she whispered. "Thanks for being my surrogate one."

Diane wiped at the corner of her eye. "Let's both stop it with the tears and eat before it gets cold."

Spoken like a true mom.

Maybe for the first time, Anna realized she was lucky to know what that felt like.

TWENTY

BLUE

Two days with hardly a word from Anna, and now he was staring down at a text message that simply read:

We need to talk.

We need to talk.

What the fuck was that?

Had he done something? Had he screwed up and—

"Blue," Frankie, their goalie coach popped his head into the locker room, "Bernard needs to see you."

"Fuck," he muttered, shoving his phone into the pocket of his slacks and stepping into his shoes. "Thanks, Frankie," he said when he passed by him in the hall where he was showing Brit something on an iPad.

They were in Seattle at the home rink of the NHL's newest team and so while the arena wasn't home, it did have quite a few perks for the visiting teams that the older rinks didn't have. In this case, it was a suite of rooms that were clean and new and state of the art, as well as several offices the coaching staff could use to chew out their players.

Which was probably on the agenda for that morning.

Blue had played like shit the previous night, directly contributing to the team's loss.

His fault. His fucking fault because he couldn't get his mind to focus on hockey, not when he knew there was something wrong with him and Anna. And that lack of focus had manifested in the form of three fucking giveaways at the blue line that had turned into easy goals for the other team.

Three.

Fucking embarrassing.

"Shit," he said, finding the room that Bernard had commandeered and knocking on the wooden panel. Time to face his doom.

"Come in."

He sucked in a breath and pushed through.

Bernard was older but in good shape, his hair fully white but his face almost unlined. He was known for his ability to scare players shitless, though he'd been a kind and fair coach to Blue from the beginning.

Today, however, with eyes narrowed and furrowed brows, he was frightening.

Or maybe that was just the sinking feeling in Blue's gut.

Had he been traded?

Fuck.

"Sit," Bernard ordered.

Blue collapsed into a chair, legs wobbling like a kid with stage fright, head spinning. Was this it? Was this the end?

Silence, for way too long given the sheer volume of his panic.

"If that leg is still bothering you, I need you to come clean with Mandy. It's too early in the season to fuck around with injuries, and we'll need you later during the playoff stretch."

Blue shook his head. "I—"

"It's either that or there's something else fucking with your mind." A brow lifted. "Maybe a problem that's in female form?"

He sighed. "My leg is fine, but my personal life is *my* business—"

"Business that's affecting the team."

Based on the previous night's game, he had a point.

Blue conceded with a nod. "It won't happen again."

Bernard shuffled some papers before stacking them together and tapping them on the desk. "See that it doesn't. You're excused from practice tomorrow. I'll see you for the game on Saturday in Vancouver."

He blinked. "What?"

"It's a short flight. Go home and take care of it. Just make sure to have your shit together when you get back."

The "or we'll have a problem" might not have been verbalized, but Blue heard the words loud and clear anyway.

"Will do."

He stood and turned for the door, pausing with his hand on the knob. "Thanks."

Bernard grunted.

Blue high-tailed it to the locker room.

He had a flight to book.

TWENTY-ONE

ANNA

She'd finally gotten the courage to text Blue, and he hadn't responded.

Nothing. Not a word or a meme or a gif.

Just radio silence that had her wondering if she'd already blown it.

"Shit," she said, tossing her textbook to the side and flopping onto her back. "I ruined it." She should have talked to him when she had the chance, not hidden in her apartment for two days straight, blowing off classes and eating nothing but Thai food delivered from the restaurant around the corner.

She hadn't even showered—the smell of her body wash made her stomach turn—and she was wearing her old, practically threadbare pajamas.

And still no word from Blue.

He was probably upset about the loss the previous night. Nobody on the Gold had played particularly well, but Blue had played particularly *bad*. Which wasn't like him in the least and what had ultimately prompted her to text. He obviously realized that something was up with her and it was bleeding over into his work.

She might be scared as hell, but she couldn't in good conscience do something that might harm his work.

And her radio silence—or bare minimum of communication in case she spilled the beans and he bolted—wasn't working.

So she'd texted.

And had hoped he would call that morning, knowing that he had two days off between games.

But he hadn't.

Maybe he'd decided to cut his losses after all.

She glanced at the pregnancy test sitting on her coffee table.

She'd bought it after seeing Diane, all gung ho and ready to face her future . . . and it had sat in its bright pink box for three days.

Cute.

Sighing, she pushed up to sitting and started to reach for the box and head for the bathroom, knowing that she could put it off no longer. It was time to face the world again—

Apparently sooner than anticipated.

Because there was a knock at the door.

Normally she would have rushed to the bathroom for her robe before answering it—hello, see-through jammies—but it was a sign of how much she was off her game because Anna simply turned, took two steps, and whipped open the door.

Then gasped and slammed it shut.

Blue.

He was there. On the other side of her door when he *should* have been in Seattle. Or Vancouver.

And she was . . . smelly and unwashed and—

"Anna," he said, knocking again, more firmly. "Open the door."

She couldn't. Because . . . OMG she just *couldn't.*

"U-uh. Just a second." She sprinted for the bedroom, tearing off clothes, yanking on new ones, trying to finger-comb her hair, and—

"Anna?"

Blue's voice was louder, as if he were—

She turned, saw that he was standing in the doorway to her bedroom, face white as he held . . . that bright pink box in his hand.

"Is—" He shook himself. "Are you—?"

She bit her lip. "I-I don't know, but I think I might be."

His jaw dropped open, the hand with the box fell to his side, and he just stared at her.

Just stayed perfectly still and stared.

For an eternity.

She lifted her chin. "I didn't plan—"

He seemed to come to life all at once. A shudder going through him as he crossed to her and gripped the outside of her arms. The cardboard bit into her skin, but she hardly felt it, not when he was looking so earnest.

"I know that," he said, brushing off one of her biggest concerns—that he'd think she'd tried to trap him—as easily as someone knocking away a fly. "Is this why you wanted to talk?"

A nod.

He crushed her to him. "Oh, baby," he murmured. "We'll figure it out together."

It was the "*we'll*" that did it.

Anna sagged against him, her own arms coming up to hold him tight as tears poured down her cheeks. "I'm sorry. I don't know how this could have happened," she sobbed.

He kissed the top of her head. "I do, sweetheart. I was there for all those orgasms, remember?"

Startled into laughter, she stared up at him. "What are we going to do?"

"First?" he asked.

She nodded.

"First, we take the test."

———

It was during the five minutes the test was processing that Anna finally found the courage to tell Blue about her parents.

She'd always thought it could come later, that she had more time to untangle the mess inside her and tell him everything.

But they didn't have any more time.

And more than that, if they were going to have a future together, Blue deserved the truth.

"I need to tell you something."

He tore his eyes from the pregnancy test, which they were both pretending not to look at, and focused on her. "Is it about your parents?"

She gaped at him. "How'd you know?"

A small smile. "Only because every time the topic of your family has come up, you change the subject. You're so good at it that it took me a long time to notice." He shrugged. "I just figured you'd tell me when you're ready."

Anna bit her lip. "I think . . . I think I'm ready now."

Fingers brushing against hers. "You sure?"

She swallowed. "Considering that we might be having a baby together?" she asked wryly. "Yeah, I think it's time you know everything."

"Okay," he said, patting the tile floor beside him. "But you have to come here while you do it. No more walls, baby."

She laughed softly but leaned more firmly against him. "My walls never had a chance with you anyway. All that barbed wire and concrete and rebar, and none of it made one bit of difference because you bombarded right through all of my barriers anyway."

He wrapped his arms around her, pulling her closer. "I prefer to think I sneaked."

"Before or after you begged me to buy you off the auction block?"

He grinned. "After. Definitely after you played the white knight." A kiss to her nose. "Now stop stalling and tell me the big secret that you think is going to get me to leave you."

Anna's jaw dropped open, and he gently closed it. "I pay attention, sweetheart, and I'm patient." One half of his mouth tipped up. "I also know what it's like to feel left behind."

Her breath caught. "*Blue*," she murmured, staring up into his eyes, seeing the truth there and . . .

She just stopped thinking.

"I love you," she said. "So fucking much, and I'm terrified because I keep thinking that once you get to know the real me, you'll discover that I'm just this frightened little kid whom nobody wanted or thought would amount to anything, and I'm just—I—I—"

Her teeth *clicked* closed, her gaze dropped to the tile.

"I love you, too," he said, stroking a hand down her hair. "And so long as the next words out of your mouth aren't: I want to raise our children as fruitarians, then *nothing* else you could say will change my mind." He put his thumb under her chin, tilted her face up so their eyes met again. "I had this vision in my head for so long, sweetheart—"

"I know," she said, pulling back. "The sweet and kind and—"

"No." A firm denial that made her heart pulse. "*No*. My vision was that for once, I wouldn't be alone."

"Oh," she breathed.

Because God yes, these last months of talking with Blue and spending time together, of having someone she was comfortable enough to text when she was feeling happy or silly or sassy . . . *fuck*, it had been incredible.

Except, for the part she'd been holding back.

Because always in the depths of her mind, she'd been too scared to hope.

But looking into Blue's eyes, seeing the openness, remembering how easily he'd bared his wounds so early on to her, gave her the clarity and understanding and strength to finally, *finally* tear off the Band-Aid.

"My parents left when I was six." She released a shaky breath. "Went to the store for milk and never came back."

"I'm so sorry," he murmured.

"I don't know if they're dead or alive or—" She shook her head. "It doesn't matter anymore."

"It matters," he said.

A nod to acknowledge him . . . and the truth that it still *did* matter, even though she didn't want it to. "I moved in with my grandmother," she said. "I was lucky because she was awesome, but then she got sick, and . . ." Anna continued, telling him how she'd continued living with her grandma for a while, until the hospital visits had lengthened, until the hospital visits had become hospice care and full time nurses, until the hospital bed had been traded for a casket. ". . . they tried," she whispered. "They really did, but there was no money. My grandmother didn't have life insurance, and anything from her estate was used for medical bills and funeral costs. I was just another expensive mouth to feed and clothe. And . . . so eventually I ended up in the system."

His hands had clenched into fists, but his hold was gentle. "Fuck, baby. I—" His voice broke. "I'm so sorry you had to go through that. D-did"—he coughed—"were you hurt?"

"Not sexually," she said, understanding what he was getting at, even without him asking the question outright. "But emotionally, yes, and physically I was assaulted a few times."

"Assaulted." One terse word released between clenched teeth. "A *few* times."

"I know it's hard to believe," she said, "but I was lucky in a lot of ways to have been older, to know what love felt like." She shook her head. "I just . . . always wondered if I'd only been a little better or nicer or sweeter . . . if maybe they would have found a way to allow me to stay."

Blue's touch was gentle as he cupped her cheek. "A little like a boy who was trying to be better so his parents would love him."

Her eyes burned because—

"Yes," she murmured. "Just like that."

He pressed a kiss to her forehead. "I am really sorry, love."

Her hand covered his. "Me, too."

They stared at each other for a long moment, but just as she opened her mouth to say, who knew what, the timer on her phone dinged.

Her heart started pounding. Her palms went sweaty.

Blue swallowed, reached for the stick. "You ready?"

Anna buried her head into his chest. "No!" A deep breath. "Okay, yes."

"One. Two. Three."

They flipped over the stick.

EPILOGUE

BLUE

"One line is negative, right?" he asked.

Anna nodded.

His gut twisted, and it wasn't disappointment. It couldn't be. Not when having an unplanned baby while they were still getting to know each other was a horrible idea.

But, dammit, it *was* disappointment.

Because Blue loved Anna and the idea of having a baby with her wasn't frightening or freak-out inducing.

It had been exciting.

He wanted that with Anna.

"Why am I sad?" she murmured.

"I don't know." He set the test on the counter. "But I am, too. Come here," he said, even though technically she already *was* there.

Anna didn't argue though, and he just held her tightly against him, his back propped against the tub, his fingers working through the tangled ends of her ponytail for long minutes. Eventually they moved to the couch, ordering food to be delivered from DoorDash and watching a reality show about glass blowing on Netflix.

They didn't talk about anything important or bring up heavy childhood memories. In fact, they didn't discuss anything more serious than whether the egg that had been crafted out of glass actually looked like an egg or if it resembled more of an *eggplant*.

Upon which the conversation turned to emojis and all their various sexual meanings, and he learned that his sexting skills were seriously lacking.

And when she finally fell asleep in his arms, Blue knew they would be okay.

———

Eight Months Later

He skated down the ice, the puck on his stick, Kevin rushing up on his left side. They were up on the Capitals, two goals to one in game six of the finals. And if they won this game, they'd win it all.

Kevin darted toward the inside and Blue floated a pass over the defenseman's stick, holding his breath until . . .

It landed, right on Kevin's tape.

A couple of rapid dekes, a flurry of small movements that faked out the goalie, and—

The goalie saved the puck.

"Fuck." More a thought than an actual word, but Blue had already been moving, sliding in to trail Kevin and provide backup. He got off a shot and . . . *shit*. Somehow, the goalie made another save.

But this time the rebound bounced out a little farther, Blue saw a flash of black, had played with Kevin long enough to know that his winger was there, and so instead of trying to stuff it home again—the goalie already moving over to cut off his angle—he used a soft touch to bump it over to Kevin.

His breath caught.

His heart seemed to stop beating and—

The puck went across the goal line.

The home crowd erupted, boisterous enough that the roar penetrated Blue's bubble of excitement.

He didn't think, just launched himself at Kevin, and they crashed into the boards, Stefan, Max, and Stevie, the third of their trio of forwards, mere heartbeats behind him. A chorus of "Fuck yeahs" and "That's rights" and well, more "Fuck yeahs," exploded around him.

But there were—he risked a glance at the Jumbotron—still two more minutes left, and so they needed to focus.

With a steadying breath, they broke apart and headed for the bench.

Blue and his linemates got a short break, just long enough to catch their breath, before Bernard sent them back out. It was brutal, his legs like lead this deep into a game and the season in general. But after all these years, they were so *fucking* close.

So he sucked it up and left it all on the ice.

Skate like hell. Check like a motherfucker. Never give up on the play.

Then get the fuck off the ice, quickly suck in some oxygen, and get the fuck back out there to do it all over again.

And all the while, the seconds counted down. A minute left.

Thirty seconds.

Twenty-two.

Fourteen.

Seven.

Three point six.

Two.

One.

!!!

Blue found himself surrounded by his teammates, knew words were being spoken, and congratulations were being exchanged and yet, he couldn't hear a damned thing.

Because they'd done it.

Somehow they'd done it.

Then the noise roared back to life, and his mind began to focus.

It only took seconds to find her. Just left of the bench, sporting the jersey with his name on it, a Gold-emblazoned beanie with a fluffy black puff on top encasing her head.

Anna.

The fucking love of his life.

He skated over to the glass, tearing off his glove to place his palm against it.

She lifted her palm, matched it to his through the glass. She had tears in those pretty blue eyes, but they were the happy variety.

"I love you," he mouthed, knowing a camera had found him, knowing the guys would give him shit later for this public display of affection, but not giving a damn.

Brit and Stefan were kissing at center ice.

That would be the bigger story by far.

"We love you," she mouthed back, her free hand lifting to cup her very large stomach.

It wasn't fat as she liked to joke, but their son, who was due to be born in just a few weeks.

Turned out they'd taken the test too early.

He wanted to take her in his arms, to hug her tight, but the fucking glass was in the way.

"Go," she mouthed. "I'll see you later."

With one more, "I love you," Blue skated back to center ice.

The Gold had a big ol' cup to receive.

Fuck. Yeah.

PR-REBECCA

Now *that* was a fucking photo op.

Blue and Anna, hands pressed together, only a layer of glass separating them, her big burly player telling his fiancée he loved her.

The hockey blogs were going to eat this shit up.

"Instagram," she murmured, fingers flying across the screen of her iPad, cropping and trimming the video into a short and snappy GIF.

Blue would hate it.

But Rebecca didn't give a damn.

This was—no pun intended—solid Gold shit.

She slapped on a filter, one that emphasized the Gold's logo on Anna's beanie, then posted the video.

"Fucking. Perfect," she said, eyes glued to her screen as she began scrolling through the rest of the camera angles and making her way to the ice. Her DSLR hung around her neck, ready to capture any high quality stills the press might miss in their effort to document hockey, rather than what was really important, at least from her perspective.

The story.

What made people care.

What turned them into lifelong fans.

What went viral.

And Blue and Anna would go viral.

Maybe Brit and Stefan, too, helmets tossed to the ice, arms around one another as they kissed full on the lips.

And all of that at center ice, music blaring, lights flashing. It was—

A fucking perfect hockey fairy tale.

Shaking her head, because she knew firsthand that fairy tales didn't exist outside of rom-coms and occasionally between alpha sports heroes and their chosen mates, Rebecca slipped through the corridor and stepped onto the Gold's bench.

Lots of dudes in suits—of both the boardroom *and* the hockey variety—were hugging.

On the ice. Near the goals. On the bench.

It was a proverbial hug-fest.

And she was the cynical bitch who couldn't enjoy the fact that the team she was with had just won the biggest hockey prize of them all.

"I knew you'd be like this."

Rebecca turned her focus from Brit, who was skating with the huge silver cup, to the man—no, to the *boy* because no matter how pretty and yummy he was, Kevin was still a decade younger than her—leaning oh so casually against the boards.

"Nice goal," she told him.

A shrug. "Blue made a nice pass."

And dammit, the fact that he wasn't an arrogant son of a bitch made her like him more.

She nodded at the cup. "You should go have your turn."

"I'll get mine," he said with another shrug.

She frowned, honestly confused. "You don't want—"

Suddenly he was in front of her on the bench, towering over her even though she was wearing her four-inch power heels. "You know what I want?"

Rebecca couldn't speak. Her breath had whooshed out of her in the presence of all that sweaty, hockey god-ness. Fuck he was pretty and gorgeous and . . . so fucking masculine that her thighs actually clenched together.

She wanted to climb him like a stripper pole.

"Do you?" he asked again when her words wouldn't come. "Want to know what I want?"

She nodded.

He bent, lips to her ear. "You, babe," he whispered. "I. Want. You."

Then he straightened and jumped back onto the ice, leaving her gaping after him like she had less than two brain cells in her skull.

The worst part?

She wanted him, too.

Had wanted him since the moment she'd laid eyes on the sexy as sin hockey god.

"Trouble," she murmured. "I'm in *so* much fucking trouble."

––––––

Thank you for reading! I hope you loved meeting Blue and Anna! The next book in the Gold Hockey series is BREAKOUT. **He was too young for her.**
A decade too young...

CLICK HERE TO READ BREAKOUT NOW>

And if you enjoyed BREAKAWAY, you'll love the sexy, sweet, and close-knit Breakers Hockey crew. The first book in the series, BROKEN, is now live!

The more she falls for Stefan, the more she risks her career... Don't miss the first Gold Hockey book. The over 400 five-star-reviewed BLOCKED is FREE!

"Off-the-charts hot, smexy scenes with one of the best book boyfriends I have come across!" —Amazon reviewer

DOWNLOAD BLOCKED FOR FREE >

I so appreciate your help in spreading the word about my books, including sharing with friends! Please leave a review on your favorite book site!

You can also join my Facebook group, the Fabinators, for exclusive giveaways and sneak peeks of future books.

SIGN UP FOR ELISE FABER'S NEWSLETTER HERE:
https://www.elisefaber.com/newsletter

———

Want a free bonus story? Hate missing Elise's new releases? Love contests, exclusive excerpts and giveaways?
Then signup for Elise's newsletter here!
https://www.elisefaber.com/newsletter

———

And join Elise's fan group, the Fabinators https://www.facebook.com/groups/fabinators for insider information, sneak peaks at new releases, and fun freebies! Hope to see you there!

GOLD HOCKEY SERIES

GOLD HOCKEY

Did you miss any of the Gold Hockey books?
Find information about the full series here.
Or keep reading for a sneak peek into each of the books below!

Blocked
Gold Hockey Book #1
Get your copy at https://www.elisefaber.com/blocked

BRIT

T he first question Brit always got when people found out she played ice hockey was *"Do you have all of your teeth?"*

The second was *"Do you, you know, look at the guys in the locker room?"*

The first she could deal with easily—flash a smile of her full set of chompers, no gaps in sight. The second was more problematic. Especially since it was typically accompanied by a smug smile or a coy wink.

Of course she looked. *Everybody* looked once. Everyone snuck a glance, made a judgment that was quickly filed away and shoved deep down into the recesses of their mind.

And she meant *way* down.

Because, dammit, she was there to play hockey, not assess her teammates' six packs. If she wanted to get her man candy fix, she could just go on social media. There were shirtless guys for days filling her feed.

But that wasn't the answer the media wanted.

Who cared about locker room dynamics? Who gave a damn whether or not she, as a typical heterosexual woman, found her fellow players attractive?

Yet for some inane reason, it *did* matter to people.

Brit wasn't stupid. The press wanted a story. A scandal. They were desperate for her to fall for one of her teammates—or better yet the captain from their rival team—and have an affair that was worthy of a romantic comedy.

She'd just gotten very good at keeping her love life—as nonexistent as it was—to herself, gotten very good at not reacting in any perceptible way to the insinuations.

So when the reporter asked her the same set of questions for the thousandth time in her twenty-six years, she grinned—showing off those teeth—and commented with a sweetly innocent "Could've sworn you were going to ask me about the coed showers." She waited for the room-at-large to laugh then said, "Next question, please."

–Get your copy at https://www.elisefaber.com/blocked

Backhand
Gold Hockey Book #2
Get your copy at https://www.elisefaber.com/backhand

SARA

"Sorry I messed up your sketch," he rumbled.

She nibbled on the side of her mouth, biting back a smile. "Sorry I stole your hand for so long."

He shrugged. "My mom's an artist. I get it."

Well, there went her battle with the smile. Her lips twitched and her teeth came out of hiding. If there was one thing that Sara had, it was her smile. It had been her trademark in her competition days.

Which were long over.

Her mouth flattened out, the grin slipping away. Time to go, time to forget, to move on, to rebuild. "Thanks," she said and extended a hand.

Then winced and dropped it when her ribs cried out in protest.

"You okay?" he asked, head tilting, eyes studying her.

"Fine." And out popped her new smile. The fake one. Careful of her aching side, she shrugged into her backpack. "I've got to go." She turned, ponytail flapping through the hair to land on her opposite shoulder.

"That—" He touched her arm. "Wait. I *know* I know you."

She froze. That was the second time he'd said that, and now they were getting into dangerous territory. Recognition meant . . . no. She couldn't.

There had been a time when *everyone* had known her. Her face on Wheaties boxes, her smile promoting toothpaste and credit cards alike.

That wasn't her life any longer.

"Thanks again. Bye." She started to hurry away.

"Wait." A hand dropped on to her shoulder, thwarting her escape, and she hissed in pain.

"Sorry," he said, but he didn't release her. Instead, he shifted his grip from her aching shoulder down to her elbow and when she didn't protest, he exerted gentle pressure until Sara was facing him again. "It's just that know I *know* you."

No. This wasn't happening.

"You're Sara Jetty."

Her body went tense.

Oh God. This was *so* happening.

"It's me." He touched his chest like she didn't know he was talking about himself, and even as she was finally recognizing the color of his eyes, the familiar curve of his lips and line of his jaw, he said the worst thing ever, "Mike Stewart."

Oh *shit*.

—Get your copy at https://www.elisefaber.com/backhand

Boarding
Gold Hockey Book #3
Get your copy at https://www.elisefaber.com/boarding

MANDY

Hockey players had the *best* asses.

No pancake bottoms, these men—and *women*—could fill out a pair of jeans. She wanted to squeeze it, to nibble it, bounce a dime—

Mandy dropped her chin to her chest, losing sight of the Sorting Hat cupcakes she'd been pondering.

Blane with his yummy ass had a unique way of distracting her.

No, it wasn't even distraction, per se. He had *always* been able to get under her skin.

And that was very, very bad for her.

"Ugh," she said, tossing her phone onto her desk and standing, knowing that she wouldn't be able to sit still now.

Nope, she needed about forty laps in the pool and a good hard fu—

Run, her mind blurted, almost yelling at the mental voice of her inner devil. *A good hard run.*

Unfortunately, the cajoling tone wasn't completely drowned out. *Some sexy horizontal time with Blane would be more fun—*

But the rest of the enticing words were lost as the roar of the crowd suddenly penetrated through the layers of concrete. Her stomach twisted. Mandy could tell, even before her eyes made it to the television, that it wasn't in celebration of a goal or a good hit either.

This was fury, a collective of outrage.

She was on her feet the moment she saw the prone form lying so still face down on the ice.

Her gut twisted when she spotted the curving line of a numeral two on the back of the player's jersey.

"Not him," she said and the words were familiar, a sentiment she had whispered, had *prayed* a thousand times before. She needed the camera angle to shift, for her to be able to see more clearly *who* was hurt. "Not him."

Then Dr. Carter was on the ice and the player moved slightly, rolling away from the camera, giving a full shot of his back and the matching twos adorning his jersey.

Fuck. Not him. Not Blane.

And that was when she saw the pool of blood.

—Get your copy at https://www.elisefaber.com/boarding

Benched

Gold Hockey Book #4

Get your copy at https://www.elisefaber.com/benched

MAX

He started up the car, listening and chiming in at the right places as Brayden talked all things video game.

But his mind was unfortunately stuck on the fact that women were not to be trusted.

He snorted. Brit—the Gold's goalie and the first female in the NHL—and Mandy—the team's head trainer—would smack him around for that sentiment, so he silently amended it to: *most* women were not to be trusted.

There. Better, see?

Somehow, he didn't think they'd see.

He parked in the school's lot, walked Brayden in, and received the appropriate amount of scorn from the secretary for being thirty minutes late to school, then bent to hug Brayden.

"I'll pick you up today," he said.

Brayden smiled and hugged him tightly. Then he whispered something in his ear that hit Max harder than a two-by-four to the temple.

"If you got me a new mom, we wouldn't be late for school."

"Wh-what?" Max stammered.

"Please, Dad? Can you?"

And with that mind fuck of an ask, Brayden gave him one more squeeze and pushed through the door to the playground, calling, "Love you!" over his shoulder.

Then he was gone, and Max was standing in the office of his son's school struggling to comprehend if he had actually just heard what he'd heard.

A new mom?

Fuck his life.

—Get your copy at https://www.elisefaber.com/benched

Breakaway
Gold Hockey Book #5
Get your copy at https://www.elisefaber.com/breakaway

BLUE

"Thanks for the ride."

"Try not to go out and get a fresh bimbo to ride tonight. I hear STIs on are the rise in the city."

Blue sighed, turned back to face her. "Really?"

She shrugged, smirk teasing the edges of her mouth, drawing his focus to the lushness of her lips. "Just watching out for Max's teammate."

He rolled his eyes. "Not hardly."

"Okay, how about I'm trying to prevent you from spreading STIs to the female populace."

"I'm clean, and I'm smart," he told her. "Condoms all the way."

"Ew."

Except there was something about the way she said it that made Blue stiffen and take notice. Because . . . he stared into her eyes, watched as the pale blue darkened to royal, saw her lips part, and her suck in a breath.

Holy shit.

"You're attracted to me."

Her jaw dropped. "No fucking way," she said, too quickly, pink dancing on the edges of her cheekbones. "You're delusional."

Blue got close.

Real close.

Anna licked her lips.

And fuck it all, he kissed that luscious mouth.

—Breakaway, https://www.elisefaber.com/breakaway

Breakout

Gold Hockey Book #6

Get your copy at https://www.elisefaber.com/breakout

PR-REBECCA

A fucking perfect hockey fairy tale.

Shaking her head, because she knew firsthand that fairy tales didn't exist outside of rom-coms and occasionally between alpha sports heroes and their chosen mates, Rebecca slipped through the corridor and stepped onto the Gold's bench.

Lots of dudes in suits—of both the boardroom *and* the hockey variety—were hugging.

On the ice. Near the goals. On the bench.

It was a proverbial hug-fest.

And she was the cynical bitch who couldn't enjoy the fact that the team she was with had just won the biggest hockey prize of them all.

"I knew you'd be like this."

Rebecca turned her focus from Brit, who was skating with the huge silver cup, to the man—no, to the *boy* because no matter how pretty and yummy he was, Kevin was still a decade younger than her—leaning oh so casually against the boards.

"Nice goal," she told him.

A shrug. "Blue made a nice pass."

And dammit, the fact that he wasn't an arrogant son of a bitch made her like him more.

She nodded at the cup. "You should go have your turn."

"I'll get mine," he said with another shrug.

She frowned, honestly confused. "You don't want—"

Suddenly he was in front of her on the bench, towering over her even though she was wearing her four-inch power heels. "You know what I want?"

Rebecca couldn't speak. Her breath had whooshed out of her in the presence of all that sweaty, hockey god-ness. Fuck he was pretty and gorgeous and . . . so fucking masculine that her thighs actually clenched together.

She wanted to climb him like a stripper pole.

"Do you?" he asked again when her words wouldn't come. "Want to know what I want?"

She nodded.

He bent, lips to her ear. "You, babe," he whispered. "I. Want. You."

Then he straightened and jumped back onto the ice, leaving her gaping after him like she had less than two brain cells in her skull.

The worst part?

She wanted him, too.

Had wanted him since the moment she'd laid eyes on the sexy as sin hockey god.

"Trouble," she murmured. "I'm in *so* much fucking trouble."

—Breakout, https://www.elisefaber.com/breakout

Checked
Gold Hockey Book #7
Get your copy at https://www.elisefaber.com/checked

"Rebecca."

She kept walking.

She might work with Gabe, but she sure as heck wasn't on speaking terms with him. He'd dismissed her work, ignored her contribution to the team. He'd made her feel small and unimportant and—

She kept walking.

"*Rebecca.*"

Not happening. Her car was in sight, thank fuck. She beeped the locks, reached for the handle.

He caught her arm.

"Baby—"

"I am *not* your baby, and you don't get to touch me." She

ripped herself free, started muttering as she reached for the handle of her car again. "You don't even like me."

He stepped close, real close. Not touching her, not pushing the boundary she'd set, and yet he still got really freaking close. Her breath caught, her chin lifted, her pulse picked up. "That. Is. Where. You're. Wrong."

She froze.

"What?"

His mouth dropped to her ear, still not touching, but near enough that she could feel his hot breath.

"I like you, Rebecca. Too fucking much."

Then he turned and strode away.

—Checked, https://www.elisefaber.com/checked

ALSO BY ELISE FABER

Checked

Coasting

Centered

Charging

Caged

Crashed

A Gold Christmas

Cycled

Caught

Breakers Hockey *(all stand alone)*

Broken

Boldly

Breathless

Ballsy (April 26,2022)

***Love, Action, Camera* (all stand alone)**

Dotted Line

Action Shot

Close-Up

End Scene

Meet Cute

***Love After Midnight* (all stand alone)**

Rum And Notes

Virgin Daiquiri

On The Rocks

Sex On The Seats

***Life Sucks Series* (all stand alone)**

Train Wreck

Hot Mess

Dumpster Fire

Clusterf*@k

FUBAR (March 29,2022)

***Roosevelt Ranch Series* (all stand alone, series complete)**

Disaster at Roosevelt Ranch

Heartbreak at Roosevelt Ranch

Collision at Roosevelt Ranch

Regret at Roosevelt Ranch

Desire at Roosevelt Ranch

***Phoenix Series* (read in order)**

Phoenix Rising

Dark Phoenix

Phoenix Freed

***Phoenix: LexTal Chronicles* (rereleasing soon, stand alone, Phoenix world)**

From Ashes

In Flames

To Smoke

KTS Series

Riding The Edge

Crossing The Line

Leveling The Field

Scorching The Earth

Cocky Heroes World

Tattooed Troublemaker

ABOUT THE AUTHOR

USA Today bestselling author, Elise Faber, loves chocolate, Star Wars, Harry Potter, and hockey (the order depending on the day and how well her team -- the Sharks! -- are playing). She and her husband also play as much hockey as they can squeeze into their schedules, so much so that their typical date night is spent on the ice. Elise is the mom to two exuberant boys and lives in Northern California. Connect with her in her Facebook group, the Fabinators or find more information about her books at www.elise-faber.com.

facebook.com/elisefaberauthor

amazon.com/author/elisefaber

bookbub.com/profile/elise-faber

instagram.com/elisefaber

goodreads.com/elisefaber

pinterest.com/elisefaberwrite